ALTERED STATEMENTS

ALTERED STATEMENTS

M.A.C. FARRANT

ARSENAL PULP PRESS
VANCOUVER

ALTERED STATEMENTS

ARSENAL PULP PRESS
100-1062 Homer Street
Vancouver, B.C.
Canada V6B 2W9

The publisher gratefully acknowledges the assistance of the Canada Council and the Cultural Services Branch, B.C. Ministry of Small Business, Tourism and Culture.

Cover illustration by Geoff Coates, used with permission
from *Adbusters Quarterly*
Author photo by Terry Farrant
Printed and bound in Canada

CANADIAN CATALOGUING IN PUBLICATION DATA:
Farrant, M. A. C. (Marion Alice Coburn)
Altered statements

ISBN 1-55152-019-2

I. Title.
PS8561.A76A88 1995 C813'.54 C95-910235-3
PR9199.3.F37A88 1995

CONTENTS

ACKNOWLEDGEMENTS

These fictions first appeared in the following magazines: "Grandma" and "Uncle Eddy" in *On Spec: The Canadian Magazine of Speculative Fiction*; "Kristmas Kraft" in *Random Thought*; "Last Campaign" and "The Department of Hope" (in a slightly different version) in *Adbusters Quarterly*; "There is a Competition for the Hearts and Minds of the People" in a shortened version in the chapbook *M A C*, produced by *fingerprinting inkoperated*; "Spin a Bible" produced by *fingerprinting inkoperated*; "Paper," "Experiments," "Addendum from the Department of Depth," "The Department of Hope," and "The Boring White Woman Lobby" in *Venue Magazine.*

"Three," originally to have been published by The Berkeley Horse (#55) in 1994, was produced as a chapbook by *fingerprinting inkoperated* in the Spring of 1995 as a memorial to David UU. With thanks to damian lopes, David Botta & Ingrid Harris.

Thanks to Terry Farrant and Pauline Holdstock for various readings of the text; to Stephen Osborne for (once again) editorial wisdom; to Brian Lam and Wendy Atkinson at Arsenal Pulp Press for production/support; to Sara Farrant for tea and sympathy; to John Costin and Mark Notte for computer help; and to Geoff Coates, creator of the cover visuals, originally an *Adbusters Quarterly* illustration for "The Department of Hope."

The support of the Cultural Services Branch, B.C. Ministry of Small Business, Tourism and Culture, and the Canada Council is gratefully acknowledged.

for
Joan Henriksen and Norman Wright

Here is the marshalling of forces. The word polishers, the format team, the paper stock . . . the stories, the lives. An army of legless people riding skateboards lead the parade. . . .

—"Sacred Tales"
from *Hiding Place of the Comediennes*

VACATION TIME

Vacation Time

Each summer during the two weeks of vacation time goldfish flee their bowls to build dazzling orange nests in trees. Monkeys, lions, and snakes trade places with accountants, lawyers, and priests, holidaying in another kind of zoo. Free birds fly voluntarily into cages allowing their rarer brothers a two-week dose of the sky. All the hard-working ants, red and black, get two weeks off to loaf on the beach. Worms crawl out of their dirty holes to hang like brown tinsel from the eaves of churches.

During the two weeks of vacation time every wronged animal is avenged: gangs of domestic cats and kamikaze budgies rampage the streets in search of juvenile delinquents; a committee of gerbils and hamsters make plans for the eradication of small boys; angry butterflies work round the clock sharpening their specimen daggers; pet turtles grow temporarily huge commanding their owners to languish in slimy tanks on the front lawn—two weeks go by and they don't feed them or change the water.

During vacation time, old women watch in horror as their pet terriers turn into porcelain dogs, as their china figurines come leeringly alive—girls with parasols, boys with fishing poles—to run off for two weeks of fragile sex in a place far away from glass cabinets.

Family Harmony

I. GRANDMA

It's unfortunate that we have to keep Grandma on the leash now when we go out for our daily walks. She's taken a sudden and dangerous dislike to other Grandmas and starts screaming as soon as she sees one. If she weren't on the leash she'd be running at them, grabbing their glasses and smashing them to the ground or else pulling at their hats and scratching their faces. Our neighbours hurry to the other side of the street when they see us coming, nodding curtly as they go by, especially if they've got their own Grandma with them.

Grandma's screaming is loud and pitched like the sound of a factory whistle. So far we've been unable to pick out any distinct words but some of the noise sounds suspiciously like the word "No!" We often wonder how it is that Grandma can sustain her screaming for so long, with barely a breath taken. It's really quite a marvel.

The screaming and straining at her leash stops as soon as the other Grandma has passed by. Turning to us she'll then begin commenting about the cherry tree in Mrs. Robert's yard, almost as if nothing has happened.

Grandma doesn't mind her leash; she'll often pat it where it lays curled up on the table as if it were a beloved dog. Sometimes she'll polish it with shoe polish, sometimes with lard, which presents a problem—it's liable to slip through our fingers. Which is what happened last Thursday. Mrs. Roberts mother-in-law, old Mrs. Roberts, was out in her front garden deadheading daffodils. She's a small, wide woman and on Thursday was bending over the bed of flowers with a pair of scissors in her hand. It's not that she meant to hurt Grandma, it's just that in her surprise when Grandma rushed her from behind, she turned suddenly with the scissors and slashed Grandma across the side of the head. (Grandma is even smaller than old Mrs. Roberts—a tiny grey person with long white hair who's fond of wearing black rubber boots.) Grandma's screaming took on a terrible pitch then and she knocked old Mrs. Roberts to the ground, wailing all the while, and punching the old woman about the head and back. It was terrible to see. It took us awhile to pry them apart because, by now, old Mrs. Roberts was fighting back and, despite arthritis, managed to stab Grandma again, this time on the hand. Blood was everywhere and the flower bed was ruined.

We told the authorities that except for the daily walk

Grandma is as normal as any other Grandma—prunes for breakfast, cream of chicken soup for lunch, a game of dominoes at four, a chop and potato for supper—but they insist that if we can't keep Grandma securely on the leash, she'll have to be taken away and locked up.

We've had a family discussion about Grandma's eccentricity and feel that the authorities are being unfair. After all, they allow old Mrs. Johnson to roam the streets in her faded red and yellow jester's costume without so much as an official scowl in her direction. And Mrs. Johnson is lewd. That costume she wears is much too small for her revealing her genitals in a most grotesque way.

And since last Thursday, the senior Mrs. Roberts has begun the peculiar habit of crouching in the rose bushes behind the fence at the front of their yard. We suspect she's laying in wait for Grandma but so far has only barked at us when we go by.

Still, we've complied with the authorities and purchased a stronger chain-link leash for Grandma, which, like her previous leather leash, she doesn't seem to mind. It's only when another Grandma crosses her vision that our Grandma loses all sense; it takes two of us to keep her reined in. If it weren't for her dogfight skills with our resident teenagers—the bloody skirmishes at the front door—we might be tempted to let Grandma wreak havoc in a home for the aged. Our daily walks would certainly be more peaceful without her. But we've decided to keep Grandma. We've come to rely on the time-honoured military tactics she adroitly uses on the teenagers—ambush, surprise attack, divide and conquer. And she's very good at blowing up their nefarious plans, too.

2. UNCLE EDDY

A small family problem we have is Uncle Eddy and the way he always disappears whenever we have visitors. Not just to his room as you'd expect from one so shy and sneaky, but down the street and across the empty field to the Dragert's backyard. Two or three days will go by before someone notices that Uncle Eddy has been absent from the dinner table. *That's right,* we say in amazement, *he's gone again!* It's only then we remember a visit from the Shrub Committee or the Mailbox Committee or the Overall Complex Committee.

The real nuisance when Uncle Eddy disappears is in bringing him back. It's got to be the same costumes every time or else Uncle Eddy won't budge from the Dragert's backyard: Father in the clown suit, the teenagers in military band attire, Grandma on her leash, of course, but wearing the purple tutu, the younger children dressed as lions, tigers, and elephants, and myself as a Kiwanis float. The dog in his special harness gets to pull the huge red wagon that is to bear Uncle Eddy home, the wagon being a recent addition because Uncle Eddy is nearing three hundred pounds and beyond our ability to carry him in the St. John's Ambulance four-hand seat as we once did.

Then, when everything is in order—we have to wait until sunset to begin, another part of the ritual—we're off, the teenagers in the lead, banging on kitchen pots or playing pretend flutes, Father bringing up the rear with Grandma and his fireman's siren.

It doesn't matter what the weather, it can be a raging

Christmas blizzard or a sultry evening in July, but to satisfy Uncle Eddy, we must proceed in the same way. As soon as we're out of the driveway it's my job to start screaming *De, De, De, De* over and over until we're reached the Dragert's backyard. Grandma says I don't call him the right way, the way she used to. *A mother knows*, she lectures. *Whatever works*, I counter, wishing we had a choke collar to go with her special chain-link leash.

You might wonder what the neighbours think. Alarm, frenzy, excitement? Not exactly. For the most part, they barely glance at us when we go by, content to remain sealed in their living rooms embracing the cool blue light of their television screens. If old Mrs. Roberts is on the loose she's liable to hurl paving stones in our direction, and that's something. But she only does this because of a recent feud with Grandma, it isn't meant as a criticism. Occasionally a few stray children and elderly people in wheelchairs will line the route—a mere two blocks—and for this reason I always carry a supply of hard candies to toss at them from the float as we go by. Once Ernest Beck, who isn't right in the head and lives in his parents' tool shed, wanted to follow along, pushing his Safeway buggy full of old newspapers and that presented a problem. There's no way on earth Uncle Eddy would come home if the parade included a stranger, even though Ernest Beck is known to everyone and snatches our newspapers regularly each morning, sometimes while we're still reading them. We've had to subscribe to even more newspapers that we already do—seven, at last count—and promise Ernest Beck we won't read them just so they'll be in pristine condition for him to pile into his cart. All this so he won't join the parade. And the Dragerts? We have to consider them because, after all, it's their backyard and if they were to get difficult, who knows where Uncle Eddy would go then. So far the Dragerts have been agreeable, claiming they never notice Uncle Eddy in their backyard. *If he's there,* they tell us, *he's as crafty as a cat.* This has the ring of truth about it because Uncle Eddy is amazingly agile for a large person. We figure it's his Wednesday night Tango lessons that accounts for this.

So you see what a nuisance Uncle Eddy's disappearance is for everyone: the sheer logistics of mounting a parade on such random notice. But the strange thing that happens as soon as we get underway is that everyone's mood turns from irritation to outright glee. We are at a loss to explain this. One minute it's all squabbling and shoving and the next, a lively carnival: the normally morose teenagers pulling out their Walkman headphones and tossing them aside in ecstasy like crutches at a revival; the smaller children cease hitting each other with 2x4s; Father gives a little more rein to Grandma's leash, for which she is so grateful she actually begins to skip; and I assume a truly regal countenance, my cardboard Kiwanis float spread about me like the enormous bulk of some queenly whale. And we always experience a mounting excitement as we near the Dragerts' yard: Will Uncle Eddy be in his usual place? What if he's not? What if we can't find him? What if he's missing for good? And when at last he's spotted where he always is—crouched, giggling, behind one of the Dragerts' rusted Fords—then it's all anxious whispers amongst us because we don't want to say the wrong thing and scare him off. Once Father yelled, *Come on out, ya brass monkey!* and Uncle Eddy wouldn't move until we went home and started the parade all over again. So we have to be careful. Usually it's Grandma or me uttering the final, gentle coaxing—*Come on, De, De, come on*—until he breaks through the tall grass, softly dusting the rust from his grey Perma-Prest slacks, and, grinning bashfully, comes towards us.

Melting everyone's hearts then because he's in such a sorry state—the crumpled suit, the dirty bald head. Gathering around and hugging him like the long lost Uncle he is, the relief all of us feel. And Grandma gently leading him by the hand to his seat in the wagon for the triumphant processional home which, fortunately, is slightly downhill or the poor dog would never make it.

Uncle Eddy is always famished after a sojourn in the Dragerts' backyard; you'd be amazed at how much he eats upon his return—ten times his normal amount—and it's got to be roast turkey and all the trimmings or watch out. And sleep! If he weren't so high up at the Bank of Commerce—where he's known as Edward J. Randall—he'd be losing his job for sure and that would be a huge problem because Father and I would have to go out to work. And if we weren't at home twenty-four hours a day making sure every little detail was looked after, what would happen to family harmony then?

3. KARMA

Karma is covered horribly with scabs. But it's all right because this is her purpose in life: to deflect the scab-causing forces meant for us. Because of Karma, the rest of the family remains scab-free. And we are grateful for this. So grateful that we overlook her more unpleasant characteristics—laziness, obesity, and nastiness, to name but three. Karma is our foster child—now twenty years old—and she's been protecting us ever since she moved in at age eleven when her adolescent personality plunged forever into a morass of spitefulness and when the scabs first appeared. We quickly became delighted with our new burden, though, when we realized Karma's unique ability to absorb the bad influences that are meant for us. Since her stay, wholesale calamity has been kept at bay.

Karma is not in pain—not obviously in pain—but she goes about her business grimly which is not surprising given the mammoth nature of her life's work. We've tried ointments and antibiotics in an effort to soothe the sores that produce her scabs, but nothing works. They are on her legs and arms, on her chest and back, and particularly on her face, that crusted, swollen face which, strangely enough, we have come to love. We use the word strangely because Karma is not a delightful person, and love only enters into the equation by the back door, because we have to love her. It's the love a hostage might feel for his tormentor, a fearful love born of necessity. Furthermore, Karma has an unpredictable nature (no doubt caused by her affliction), sometimes docile, sometimes—let us say—nastily forceful. We never know if it's a plate of french fries she's wanting, or a new load of wool. And if it's wool, what colour this time, what weight? The wool is for the crude afghans which Karma knits while watching TV. Our furniture and beds are covered with them. We use them as wall hangings and as rugs. There are so many afghans we're smothering in them. (If she'd only let us give them away!) She's currently fond of a putrid shade called Cinnamon Dust and if we can't find this shade in the department stores. . . .

And so we're careful with Karma and put up with her tantrums. Because though she's sullen and never smiles, though she's liable to smack the younger children when she's hungry or pounce on the resident Grandma whenever she ventures upstairs in search of sugar or an egg to borrow, we do not admonish her. The truth is we are afraid to now. Who knows what scab-causing forces would befell the family once and for all if Karma were to move out and get an apartment of her own? She threatens this every time we forget to buy her weekly supply of Black Magic chocolates.

But move out permanently? Don't even suggest it. It's bad enough what we endure when Karma stays with Ernest Beck in his tool shed. Slimy, nothing-in-the-head Ernest Beck, smelling like gasoline and years-old body dirt living miserably in his parents' tool shed. What she's doing in there with him doesn't bear imagining but sometimes she stays for a week at a time. When this happens the whole family becomes alarmed. Because bad things begin to occur: someone trips and falls down the basement stairs, or a boiling kettle is knocked off the stove, causing surface burns to a passing child. But these are minor irritations, trifling things, nothing for the emergency ward. Everything's just fine, we assure each other. Just a few scrapes. Happens to every family. Disaster hasn't made an appearance yet. Catastrophe still doesn't know our name. All the while watching nervously out the kitchen window for Karma's return.

It's not until Karma has been absent for longer than twenty-four hours that our serious worrying begins. Because if she's gone longer than a day this is what happens: the household machinery has a seizure. What was once a wonder of mechanical efficiency during Karma's residence suddenly turns sinister and refuses to serve us: the vacuum cleaner might explode in a flash of white light, the living room end tables collapse for no apparent reason, the book shelves vomit forth dusty titles. Not long after this the cars in the driveway succumb: mufflers clatter to the gravel, radiators clog and choke, fanbelts fly off without provocation.

Three days into Karma's absence and the family pets get horrible puss-filled sores, not unlike Karma's own. (We dare not think they are replacement sores.) This means costly visits to the vet and operations, antibiotics, and a great deal of worry about the well-being of our cat and dog. Because once the sores begin, the cat's brain infection isn't far behind. This happens if Karma is gone for four days. As soon as the cat starts oozing a foul-smelling liquid from his eyes and ears we know the worst has come—Sweetie 16 is about to succumb and the frantic search for her replacement, Sweetie 17, must begin. The fourth day is also the day the dog's testicles begin to shrivel and flake like dandruff, leaving a sad, miserable trail along the living room rug. So far the dog has endured Karma's absences (unlike the cats), but he's a stoic, humourless dog and finds run-and-fetch games now completely beyond him. Of course, we know what's going on and it's dismal to see: the poor animals just aren't strong enough to take over Karma's work. We understand this; it takes someone as resolutely miserable as Karma for so important a job.

On the fifth day the youngest children become listless, refusing all food and television entertainment. When this happens we get deeply scared. Because it's only a matter of moments before the first bone breaks (usually an ankle or wrist). And it always happens in surprising ways, never how you'd expect—from roughhousing, or swinging from trees. It happens like this: quietly, of its own accord. Their bones will simply start snapping. Which is what happened to William after Karma's last absence—felled reaching for butter at the breakfast table. Another green stick fracture of the tibia, his eighth. The sound of breaking bones is exactly like the crack of kindling being readied for the fire. A sound we've come to hate.

At this juncture, we pay a visit to Ernest Beck's tool shed. We're not beneath begging Karma to return because if we're at the sixth day, it's likely the ear and eye infections will soon begin. Miserable, scream-causing infections, projectile vomiting. Why does the world hate us?

Of course, we're always hoping that Karma will return of her own accord. We like to think the "love" and appreciation we feel for her is mutual. And sometimes she does return before the sixth day, sometimes she's only gone for the afternoon or overnight so no harm is done. But if it's the sixth day, even though we're desperate, we're pretty certain that Karma is sick of Ernest Beck by now and agreeable to returning. This is because Ernest Beck doesn't have a TV in his shed and he doesn't provide Karma with chocolates and cheesecake the way we do. So we fill the red wagon with boxes of Black Magic chocolates, fudge brownies, Big Macs and french fries, and the latest edition of *Bride Magazine* (her favourite). Then we place the wagon outside the door of the tool shed. It's only a matter of moments before the smell of the Big Macs reaches Karma inside. Imagine our delight when the door explodes open, and our huge protector appears, muumuu dishevelled, nose twitching, eyes wild until she spies the wagon. Ernest Beck can take a hike then. Ernest Beck has about as much importance as a cockroach then. We've seen her topple him with one arm in her lunge for the wagon. At this happy juncture we know our household is on the sure road to recovery.

Our idea of heaven is this: Karma's back home and settled on the chesterfield watching cartoons. She's knitting another brown afghan and there's a bag of Thunder Crunch and a two-litre bottle of Coke beside her on the newly-repaired end table. We like to gather the family together and behold Karma at this time, giving prayerful thanks. Often at night when the lights are off and only the TV set flickers, Karma's encrusted face can be seen in profile, illuminated by the light of the television screen. If she suddenly shouts and clutches her arm or her chest we are at first alerted and then profoundly relieved: we know that another evil wind has just blown through the walls in our pursuit, and that Karma is busy at work fending off our demons, our doom. Adding another scab to her heavily burdened back. We know the family is safe. For the time being.

Yes Made Famous

I was behind again with the payments. The credit card reps had called so many times they used up the tape on my answering machine. The numbers to call back! Seven digit numbers, ten if you include the area codes, a flurry of 1-800s. I entered the numbers in a blue-lined accounting book. Then added them up. The total was 952,297,646,801. I thought: This is too much to owe anyone, never mind that they're telephone numbers. I thought: This is too great a number to be accountable for.

The taped voices of the credit card reps said, Please, said, Call us, said, Twenty-four hours a day. Who else would be so generous with their time? Young, soft-sounding men with names like Kevin, Christopher, and Troy, surely with mothers, maybe in possession of mothers who are overdue just like me.

That I'm overdue, there's no denying. Oh, seriously, terminally. I won't give you an argument; I'm over my limit.

To the reps who reached me live, I said, What's it like being a credit card rep? Is the pay any good? Are they taking applications? I said, Do you ever speak to your mother about these things?

This tactic works well with telephone solicitors. Telephone solicitors like diversion. When they call asking to clean my chimney or give me a prize, I ask about conditions at work. I'm so sympathetic. Are they required to sit in tiny booths for hours on end? Do they feel like assembly line chickens, hemmed in, without regular breaks for exercise? Do they receive a wage or is it just commission? And how do they manage, how do they make ends meet? Many a solicitor wants to talk. I'm a crisis line in reverse for people who don't know they need a crisis line. The stories I've heard: You're right, the leg cramps are awful. . . . The pay's lousy but what can you do, I've got two kids. . . . If only we didn't have to eat.

It's the same with door-to-door salesmen. Oh please! I say, and ask them in. Such scruffy, sad boys. Sure, give me the free clean, try out your stuff. Here, have a cookie, a cup of tea. Is the pay okay? Are you making any sales? And then my personal reservoir of pity is unleashed. The vacuums I've bought!

But the credit card reps are too swift for loose sympathy. They're professionals, trained to manoeuvre like assassins: merciless, one-track, no nonsense. They may sound beguiling but they've got your number, they mean business. And they love their work. Feel good, feel morally wonderful when they tell you this: It's your own damned fault, you've spent too much.

A truth: I can't help myself; I've spent too much. This life is full of truths but they're not the truths I'm wanting.

Recently I went into a store called Window Dressing. The inventory was staggering. So many little things! Scented candles, small picture frames made of wood, coloured bottles, linens in lovely colours—wine, green, silver, cobalt blue. Christmas ornaments in gold and white—stars, moons, porcelain angels. The place full of women in their fifties, heavily ringed, gold-chained, wearing the finest corduroy slacks in muted shades of green, pink, and taupe. Signing up for courses in dead flower arranging, buying wrought iron candelabras to show off their home-made candles, collecting beige silk roses to stick in their summer hats. Oh, to be one of those unburdened women! Who love their crafts so well. Another truth: there's a fleet of bright, happy women out there sewing up pot holders in costly prints to put under your tree at Christmas.

This store has a newsletter! If you get on their mailing list they'll give you a free false flower with every purchase.

I signed up.

I could do with a free false anything.

I bought twelve cotton dinner napkins, white with gold embroidery. Suitable, the tag said, for special occasions.

Of course they're useless. Pretty but useless. Good for fondling. For the furtive caress in the linen drawer. Because at my house, dinner parties are an endangered species. Let me put it another way: they're beyond endangered, they're extinct.

All right, I'm talking about love. Love took a hike. Called it quits. Took the last craft show ornamental sleigh out of town. What I mean is, my beloved and I manoeuvre around each other like trained assassins.

It's reassuring to know I have a sickness. This helps. Not much, but a little. I go to the meetings, Tuesday nights. Seven women, one man. And the leader, Jerry. One by one we get up and say this: My name is Verna (Carol, Arlene, Joy, Debbie, Katherine, Wendy, Clint) and I'm a Shopaholic.

You heard it right. Shopaholic.

We Shopaholics can't stop buying; it's got to do with a poverty in our souls. This is Jerry talking. Soul is a big word these days, an old star on the comeback trail, a has-been idea enjoying a revival. Once again everyone has a soul but it's the new, improved variety. Say goodbye to God.

Between God and our newly-created souls what we had was credit, buying power, and the lovely coolness of things.

A brief golden age, I'm convinced. One day they'll tell stories about all the wonderful things we had.

Jerry is full of soul. His brown eyes brim with it. His moist hands drip with it. A recovered Shopaholic, wearing old grey slacks, a Goodwill sports jacket, holes in his soles. Of his shoes, that is. Jerry has stopped buying. Stopped buying! His story: the crisis always comes. Sooner or later. The great face-the-music crisis when there's nothing left to spend, and everything to owe.

One of my live credit card reps said as much. Verna, he

said, think about us: we let you have all that money and now we want it back. Jonathan was his name. A nice boy, said he'd just made assistant supervisor. I asked him where his office is. Vancouver, he said. God's country.

I'm a new member of Shopaholics Anonymous; you can always tell the new members, we look like we live in this world—chic, up-to-date. (I bought a new coat for the first meeting.) Old members look like Jerry. Like bag people with soul.

An attitude which is not good for my soul, I'm told. Which is in tatters, I'm told. You're replacing your need for love with things, Jerry says. That's the idea. If I want to find my soul—cure my sickness!—he says, the cynicism and the spending have to go.

But I love buying things, I said, I'm a flasher with plastic; it's so reliable; anytime I want to feel good, voila! Jerry and the seven other members looked sad when I said this, and shook their heads. You're a slave to the consumer society, they told me; wake up and smell the burning plastic.

Lay me out in a see-through coffin: I'm Verna and the seven Shopaholics.

Anytime we get the urge we're supposed to phone. We're supposed to help each other resist these phrases: *Prices slashed! Fifty to seventy percent off! Sale ends Thursday!*

Jerry has another message: deconstruction. Because everything can be taken apart. He tells us to take out our notebooks. Our meetings are held in the basement of Holy Trinity

Church. Where else? Upstairs: the old idea of soul with it's beard and cane goes creaking about. Downstairs: the New Year's Baby soul sits in dirty diapers.

Irony is another thing that has to go.

Jerry tells us to deconstruct the act of buying. List the steps from thought to purchase, pick apart our need. Because like all addicts we're driven to find fulfillment in self-destructive ways. If we can gain mastery over the parts of our addiction then what we get is freedom.

Freedom to be empty. This is what I'm scared of. If I can't buy things—if I don't have my beloved's love—then I'm a warehouse full of nothing.

This is what we Shopaholics are addicted to buying:

Carol (age 55): major appliances
Arlene (age 78): wool (to date, 1,915 afghans)
Joy (age 33): lingerie, particularly silk
Debbie (age 41): a generalist, anything, everything
Katharine (age 69): ornaments, with a fondness for Spode
Wendy (age 47): sportswear, especially aerobic wear
Clint (age 35): with a sly interest in Joy (the person, not the state)—books and computer software
Verna (age 42): My addiction takes this form: I love the homey feeling I get shopping for household items. Tea cosies, linens, throws for the chesterfield. Chesterfields! Decorator towels, down quilts, duvet covers, touch lamps, swivel lamps, pine tables, bone china. Persian

rugs! I love creating a place of warmth, breathing life into cold rooms. Cold hearts.

The crisis came. Inevitably. Like the freeway truck gone berserk that we all know about. Like two trucks; it was a dual crisis. First the credit card drought, then this: he, grumbling about boxer shorts. All right, his name is Duncan. Duncan's exact words were: Jesus, the elastic's gone on another pair. Then the jowly glare in my direction. What? What? I screamed. I'm now responsible for the state of your underwear?

I told this story to my Tuesday night group, my contribution to the picking-apart exercise Jerry had us do. But by then I'd made it so funny I was having trouble getting the words out.

I bought forty-four pairs of boxer shorts, a pair for each year of his life. Picture the marriage bed heaped with shrink wrapped packs of boxer shorts—plaid flannel ones, silk ones, yellow cotton ones with happy faces, distinguished striped polyester ones.

Not funny, said Jerry. The others said: pathetic.

Strike sense of humour from the list of things I can no longer buy.

Did Duncan find it funny? Jerry asked.

Well, no, not exactly; he called it the last straw.

At this juncture, Clint, recently separated, read something aloud from a novel: *In its worst state, the traditionally married are battling, shrieking, and occupying each other's brains like some terrible tumour until one of them dies.* When he was through reading he smiled at us aggressively. Jerry patted my hand, damply. Tears are best, he said.

Carol, a bankrupt woman who once possessed a garage full of washing machines—who once possessed a garage—put the Shopaholic theme song on the old portable record player. The Beatles. What else? *Money can't buy me love.*

We tapped our feet, nodded our heads sadly to the music. Pathetically.

I'm facing the music and what I hear is Mozart's *Requiem* and the famous Chopin dirge. Also cash registers struck dumb in my presence and the scissor-snap of waiters cutting up my holy trinity of cards: Visa, Amex, MasterCard. Nasty waiters annointing my Pasta Supreme with plastic shards.

What I hear is Duncan's solo fugue, his aria fugata, his discordant declaration: I've had it with you Verna; what you need to recover from is life!

Next comes inspiration. Jerry told us the proud story of Karen, a Shopaholic graduate. He called it his Double Eyelash Story.

Karen was a woman who looked great with her make-up on and terrible when it was off. You wouldn't know it was the same person, he said. She was so beautiful when she was made up and with her blonde hair—always styled and never with the roots showing—and her perfect clothes, she was a real knock-out. When she got married she wore two sets of false eyelashes on each eye. Her husband Harlan told her: if you're going to look like that at our wedding, you're going to look like that all the time. He said: If I'm marrying a woman who wears two sets of false eyelashes—looking great, mind you, there's no denying that—then I want her to look like that all the time. So after the wedding Karen would get up each morning two hours before her husband just to put on her make-up. Not only the two sets of false eyelashes, but foundation, shadow, blush, the whole works, transforming herself into this magazine-perfect face to stare at her husband with across the breakfast table, day after day, month after month. And, of course, she got herself into serious debt over this, buying all that make-up, getting so obsessed with trying to please her husband that she couldn't stop buying. She bought everything. Maybe he'll like my face better as a Cover Girl or a Revlon is how she explained her addiction to herself. And then she branched out into perfumes, body lotion, bath oils, and wigs. It's no wonder she turned to drugs. Because, of course, by now, Harlan's love was waning, and no matter how often she changed the made-up look of her face, or how much she altered her image, she couldn't recover his attention. Her crisis came with an overdose of cocaine. And shortly thereafter—at the suggestion of a hospital counsellor—she joined Shopaholics Anonymous. That was four years ago. Thanks to the guidance she received from us, she's since paid off her debts and divorced Harlan. In fact, I saw her on the street a couple of months ago. She's opened up a health food store. She was wearing a long flowered skirt and Birkenstocks, you know the look. Her hair all mousy brown, no make-up, and definitely no double eyelashes. You wouldn't know it was the same person. A real business woman, but plain-looking.

Come into my store any time, she told me, I'll give you a real deal on pinto beans. In her spare time Karen has become a champion of the Shopaholic message, touring schools and giving talks in community halls. It's the least I can do, she told me, I'm that grateful.

If Karen could control her addiction, Jerry told us, we can too.

At the last meeting of Shopaholics Anonymous we had to take out our checkbooks and with Magic Markers draw heavy black lines across each cheque. Then those of us whose credit cards hadn't already been slashed were handed a pair of large cutting shears. One by one we faced the group and, with scissors held high in one hand and a credit card in the other, declared loudly: Cash only! Cash only!

A kind of ecstasy overcame us. Cash only! everyone chanted, rising from their chairs and dancing about the room.

Verna, Jerry said, putting a sweaty hand on my shoulder (I thought he was asking me to dance). Verna, Verna, he said soothingly, we love you.

The heavy-hearted love of Jerry and of Carol, Arlene, Joy, Debbie, Katherine, Wendy, and Clint. I'm not sure it's love I want.

This is something I did yesterday at home. It was the day the men from Furniture City repossessed our blue velvet Kroehler chesterfield with matching love seat, and our mahogany coffee table. *(Don't pay for one full year!)* They were in and out of the house in five minutes, wouldn't even stop to chat. I'd wanted to know if they were union workers, if there was a limit on how much weight they could carry. But they were in such a rush I couldn't get an answer. The older man was heavy set, balding, wore glasses, looked something like Duncan. On his last trip out the door I grabbed his arm and asked him if he found his work emotionally draining, were there times when he just had to question the ethics of what he was doing?

Lady, he said, I don't feel nothing.

What I did when the men from Furniture City left was to deconstruct love. Duncan's and my love. What there is left of it. I sat myself down on the bare carpet, took out my Shopaholic's clipboard and listed the steps of love, noting our sad journey from first hot glance in 1981 to final glare last week. I went year by year, through all fourteen years, listing gifts exchanged and their relative worth, listing major compliments and criticisms traded, and I rated each year's lovemaking on a scale from one to ten (the score sliding with each year—oh, a silent killer, sliding, sliding!). I picked apart everything. Who did what around the house, who contributed more to romance.

And I came to understand this: I'm about to be toppled by last truths.

Last truth #1. No amount of freshly bought household items can now scale the forbidding mountain of Duncan's back turned away from me in bed.

Last truth #2. The truth of my addiction: it's the famous

yes made famous. What I've come to call the declaration of love. The great beatific booming nod that says yes to the world. Yes. Yes. Yes. Yes. And yes.

All right, I'm empty. I've scraped and scraped away at this thing, I've gone through all the layers, and what I'm covered with is nasty shards, broken bits of love.

I've come clean.

If this was a stick-up there'd be an accusing finger pointing at my brand new soul. There'd be a bound and gagged woman still struggling to buy Duncan one last gift, something that would nudge him gently from no to yes. The gift of a different kind of music, perhaps. Something bright and light-stepping with flutes and drums, and with a chorus of singers strewing flowers, dancing gaily ahead.

ARK

Ark

For the escape we took everything we needed, even the beach sand which was receding quickly from the shoreline around our town.

In our cabin on board we tacked up all the old mementoes: the 8x10 pictures of your recreational hockey team; pictures of our daughter at ages one through seven; all the various licences—marriage, birth, fishing, burning; and two copies of every tax notice we'd ever received. We posted all the calendars from all the years as a reminder that we had lived; each month marked off with events attended: meetings, appointments, parties, lessons, funerals, the Boilermakers' Ball.

We remembered everything: the filing cabinets filled with bank statements and the proofs we'd paid our bills—the invoices marked "balance nil," the cancelled cheques—hydro, cable, tele-

phone, garbage—and credit card statements with congratulations for servicing our burgeoning debt. We took rent receipts and mortgage statements, and insurance policies no longer valid for car and house, dismemberment, earthquake.

We took all the letters we'd ever received, and birthday cards, Christmas cards, and cards reminding us of life's memorable events—graduations, valentines, sickness, death. The cards listed alphabetically and filed according to year, with special sections for those containing humour, and for those that made us blink and stare.

We took our symbolic discourse: memos, directives, communications, press releases; we took our colourful bulletins sporting twelve kinds of fonts. And piled them loosely beneath the port hole.

In the adjoining bathroom we stacked our reading material: magazines, comics, brochures, contracts, reports and missives, documents, and deeds. We took one hundred books on how to enrich our lives and that study in handsomeness, the Oxford Bible, a farewell gift from your mother in the home. And The Five Thousand Secrets of Sister G., *we took that too, a splendid book promising enough secrets to last our lives.*

When we reached our destination we stripped the cabin bare; it was like moving house—things got broken, things got lost. There were books and papers everywhere, and stacks of sand piled in boxes beside the door. We lost time looking at old photographs; our daughter fell off the gangway and had to be saved; there was a shortage of empty cardboard boxes. Our chief worry became how to unload our things onto the dock; there was no one to help. Beach sand was spilling everywhere, each box weighed a hundred pounds. We suffered heat and flies, and the strange and curious natives with their greedy, outstretched hands.

Still, our faith and our optimism remained. We carried our copy of The Guidebook to a Near Life Experience, *it bravely pointing the way.*

The Miss Haversham Club

The doctors have declared: all women over the age of sixty-five are now to take daily hormone supplements. They're sick sick sick of dealing with brittle bones, snapping bones, bones splintering under the glare of moonlight, bones shattered from sneezing, pounding carpets, pouring tea. All those studies, they cry. And correlations! And don't forget the important womb-removal work on younger women which must continue at all cost; my God, they add, those thousands of useless bones have been interfering with that! So it's mandatory now—megadoses of estrogen and testosterone each morning with tea.

But the doctors are blind to the side effects, the shocking transformation of our old women. A geriatric plague has been unleashed and it's not the plague we expected.

This is how it's become: old women fleeing their homes, banding together in terrible gangs, roaming the malls and city streets with lust and revenge in their hearts. We're in the midst of an elderly sex epidemic and we fear for our men. Few of them are safe. Old men who would normally be lapping up attention are scared silly and lock themselves away in their rooms; younger men won't venture out on the streets alone. Even our own Grandma—that small, solemn figure—helpless before her exploding libido, escaped into the night wearing nothing but her flannel dressing gown and moccasin slippers. We haven't seen her for five months and she's ignored all our newspaper ads: *Grandma call home—we love you.*

The Grandma Gangs, as they've come to be called, are everywhere now—fifteen or twenty at a time, umbrella'd, in their Adidas track shoes and pastel jogging suits, stalking lone men in underground parkades, on darkened streets. And braying at the moon, they are—we've seen it on the nightly newscasts—crowds of them gathered outside the beauty shops at midnight, wearing their new chemical virility like a sacred shawl. Singing those dreadful hymns: The Hymn of Ancient Vaginas, The Hymn of Stolen Ovaries. Oh Oh Oh. Then there's the new, sinister brand of geriatric PMS and the violence the old women are inflicting on our public statues: defacing Sir John A's privates; the unknown soldier smothered in Vaseline; rubber dildos dangling from the memorial guns.

It's got to stop. Because listen to this: one hundred and thirty-seven old women inmates at Shady Creek Nursing Home have taken hostages. They're on the roof waving canes, hurling walkers at onlookers below. Three male orderlies have been bound and molested and the old women say it's only a matter of time until the rest of the staff gets the same treatment. What they want: support groups for octogenarian mothers and truck loads of government-supplied sanitary napkins. *You try living on a pension and buying those things,* they scream from the rooftops.

Where will it end? Rival splinter groups battle each other outside our buildings of commerce. The Recharged Bosom Club wearing black satin bras. The Miss Haversham Club in their rotting wedding gowns, trailing cobwebs. It's territory they're after, and the pin-striped accountants, bankers, and financial advisors who grace our streets like stiff ballerinas each day at five. Never before has their scurry from pillar to post been so threatened.

Stop them. Stop the old women, we plead. Take back the hormones. Give them to cows, chickens, to anyone but Grandmas. Is anybody listening? We want our old women returned to us; we have need of their counsel, of their wise and tender ways.

But the doctors refuse to comply—all those wombs and the numbers gleefully climbing. And the medical conglomerate is overjoyed. Overjoyed! Bone business down, pharmaceuticals up! The city fathers are useless. Pleading committee, pleading next month, next year, next century. Armoured vehicles for their personal use.

Meanwhile the good citizens are adding Grandma Gangs to their list of postmodern woes. A terrible thing has been unleashed, a monster. Even the slimy delinquents shrink beneath the old women's fury: *Behave you little stinkers,* the women scream at them, *or we'll rip off your balls!*

The Finishing Symphony

A man has two heart attacks in succession like shock waves, then a third, a cracking earthquake heart that fells him. He lays on a hospital bed in his doctor's office, in the waiting room, a warning to the other patients to quit smoking, go easy on the fried foods.

The doctor has in mind an aura of pallor: a grey-skinned body gasping for air, a loathsome death.

But before a week is up, the sick man is feeling better. He's torn off his wires and tubes, and is sitting up in bed reading magazines, chatting with the waiting patients, calling for visitors.

As a gesture of solidarity his many friends gather at his bedside wearing night gowns, pyjamas, T-shirts and underwear; a few of them are naked. The mood turns festive and a catering outfit is called in to supply sliced meats and cheeses, rye bread, pickles; the delivery men join the party. The waiting patients join in too: an arthritic old man with stomach pains, a child with earache, two pregnant woman, a soccer player on crutches, a woman suffering from constipation. Several interns who are training with the doctor dance together in bare feet and operating gowns. The doctor's receptionist has turned up the Muzak—a string section plays the road theme from *Easy Rider.*

The sick man is delirious with joy. Kneeling on his bed and waving his arms, he's conducting the party, a *Bourree For Sick Man And Friends,* a finishing symphony. The old man passes around a bottle of gin.

The party carries on well into the night. In the small hours, the revellers wrap him in hospital sheets, cheering, singing, and push his hospital bed through the deserted streets.

The sick man yearns for stoplights and traffic—the neon whiz of rushing cars. They head toward a freeway intersection. Then it's rain he wants, with brake lights glowing on wet pavement. As if on cue, a misty rain descends. Still not satisfied, the sick man declares: *Car lots! But they must be deserted at three a.m. and brightly lit, with rows of coloured hoods hunched like impatient racers—with plastic flags snapping in the wind.* The revellers race with the bed down back streets until they find a car lot on the outskirts of town.

Oh, it's all so beautiful, the sick man cries, *but there's one more thing: one of those cold beacons of hope, an all-night grocery store. It's a tired worker I want, sitting on a stool behind the counter in an empty store, a mat of lottery tickets before him, and videos, cigarettes, pop to sell and it's four a.m. and no one's buying.*

When they return to the doctor's office it's dawn; the sick man says he's feeling good. But then suddenly he complains of an oily feeling, his feet feel like asphalt. Beads of oil start oozing from the soles of his feet, breaking like sweat from his forehead, upper lip, neck and armpits. He collapses, barely breathing.

The doctor rushes to his bedside; vital signs are checked, the pulse is weak but the hoped-for deathly pallor is still missing. *Damn it, man,* the doctor cries, e*ither die or get well, I've about had it with you!*

Last Campaign

He instructed me to get a copy of his favourite television commercial. Which I did. The one with the twin teenaged girls selling chewing gum—in their bathing suits beside the pool, enticing identical boys with their smiles.

I then cut the tape into bite-sized portions, as he requested, and heaped the bits onto a white dinner plate. Next, I poured Creamy Garlic salad dressing over the entire lot and fed it to him, one forkful at a time, while standing beside the maroon leather chair across from his Executive desk. I was completely naked. He wore his grey slacks and his new lemon yellow sports shirt. We were in our sunny office, the front one with a fine view of the parking lot.

The tripod, which stood five feet away, held the Pentax.

With the remote control attached to his foot, he took the picture. We were after the Helmut Newton effect: the mannequin-like model, naked, red lips, high heels—the bizarre and dangerous juxtaposition.

Except for the visual distractions of the coffee maker, the filing cabinets, and the trophy fish behind the desk, the picture turned out quite well. We are planning to feature it on the front cover (full-bleed) of the Spring Flyer. We believe it will stand out from all the other flyers which will soon be circulating through the mail and as newspaper inserts, grabbing market attention in a significant way.

Our children and grandchildren are quite supportive of just what might be our last advertising campaign. After all, the business is their inheritance and, for the past while, business has not been good. We are hoping, therefore, to revive sales in a dramatic way. Not only that, but to avoid staff layoffs as well. Some of our employees have been with us for over thirty years. We have told them we will do whatever is necessary to save their jobs: we appreciate our responsibility and will not wither from it.

Right now the employees are huddled together in wretched hopefulness outside the office door. We, in here, are going over final proofs for the Spring Flyer cover. We think it may have a profound impact on the local community: NAKED GRANDMOTHER SELLS POCKET WRENCHES! The publicity can only help us.

Thunder Showers in Bangkok

Sitting on these front steps. Two drunks go by saying my name. Hello, you two, hello.

They were all there, all the important ones, on the cover of the final issue: Mina Holland, George Van, Howard Curtail. The three of them looking solemn, standing full-faced before the camera, posed on a freeway overpass. Cars and trucks behind them, indistinct, a blur, a streak of grey because of the slow exposure. And only the poets in focus, as if they'd stepped out of time, walked away from the murky world. The photograph in black and white, the magazine title and their names printed in red.

I was living in a third-floor room then, on the corner of

Railway and Fourth. People from the old days dropping by to read their works. One we particularly admired, though his output was small: John Savage, or Savage John as he called himself then. We knew him for his warmth and accessibility but that was only one extreme. His work was marked by bleakness and we spent many hours talking of this, how this could be so. I felt that the bleakness was true and said how we are always on the edge and that this is the truest reality—knowing as much about this life as we are able to bear. After that we become giddy and drunk and must have the necessary moments of forgetfulness. This thought became the theme of the final issue, the preface, a quote from Lorca: *Life is laughter amidst a rosary of deaths.*

Years later John Savage was found dead on the 401, the top of his head shaved off but clutching that last important work. He'd had a part-time job washing down the freeway at night. Tough work but possessing the right amount of scrab. Scrabbing was what we were about—the low-lying, lizard-crawling belly living where we found our poems. The diving deeply, the geyser quest. And we put out the journal whenever we could. *Thunder Showers in Bangkok,* we called it, because that was right too.

In those days we'd mine the junk heaps of this miserable city, finding our poems in the grimiest of places. Creating our jewels from the trash of the age. At times we'd read in the lobby of the public library to the street people and the mentally confused gathered there for the warmth. Or hold poetry festivals in church basements where maybe three or four strangers would attend. I read a poem called "Beige" at a highly promoted reading. There were two people in the audience. Afterwards one of them said, Beige, that's interesting, I once saw a movie that was beige.

Little by little, we witnessed the death of the literary age.

And now?

Cities are dying for lack of what we were able to say.

Electronic wizardry is everything.

And we find ourselves committed to very small acts, hoping to find a manageable content, some link, some rope to swing on. Reduced to servicing our intense inverted passions because out there is so unknowable.

Ordinary reality is not all there is and, to put it bluntly, is something of a bore. Breton said that, or maybe it was Blake. It doesn't matter. This is the end of the twentieth century and we like to mix things up, everything from all the times frothing together in a crazy late life stew. And so I've arrived on these steps where I spend my days watching the drunks go by. Didn't use to be so many drunks, now they're going by all the time. The eternally stunned, the eternally confused. And I'm living in slow time. Even without a watch I know the hour, the day, almost to where the moment is tethered. The rest of the world is beyond me, an indistinct blur, in nanosecond time.

This work of enlarging the orb. I've spent my life at it.

As my farewell to the world I'll compose an engaging little partita set in a minor mode. Composed while still scrabbing in the slow time of existence. As a tribute to those who have gone before me, to those who are no more. I've learned this much: to be human now is to partake of a cult existence.

Two drunks go by saying my name. Hello, you two, hello.

Don't bother sketching in a past for me, the two-step to this final step. That's sociology. Cause and effect. That's all about redemption. I've become part of the equation that takes five billion particles to balance. In other words, I have my place. Call it betwixt. There's a word—between two states. The twin pillars. The doorway to light guarded by two miserable hounds.

The last copies of *Thunder Showers in Bangkok* are stacked beside my bed. Buried treasure in a handful of words.

There's a tour bus leaving every half hour from the station. You won't want to miss it. Word has it that tonight the children will be violating the city. Some as young as eight, none older than fifteen. Several of their crowd are supposed to be hanged in Memorial Park. Something to do with a bushfire of bad feeling.

Innocence

Our dinner was disturbed by the sight out the window. A large missile shaped like a child's transformer toy hovered there, emitting sparks as if in preparation for a deadly strike. We watched, afraid that it might malfunction and destroy us by mistake when we had finally got our lives in order, found love, rearranged our families, brought together under the same roof children who were once strangers to each other—your two boys, my two boys. All this so we could love in peace. The former husband bitterly exiting through five cities then neatly dying in a plane crash. The former wife never mentioned.

All this accomplished and now the threat of annihilation hovering outside the window like a judgment about to deliver just desserts, retribution, come-uppance.

We fled, of course. The six of us in the car trying to outrun the thing. We thought we'd succeeded when we hit the freeway. But looking back saw that the hovering had ceased and the missile had begun moving towards us, lower and lower through the sky. Then the smaller section on its shaft fell away—the signal that it was about to activate and seek its mission. By now we understood that we were not its present target, although the missile came close to grazing the roof of our speeding car.

Before dinner the next night you showed our new family a video you'd taken of yourself in a sports outfit and clown wig, kicking a soccer ball across an open field. *Create a video of yourself which your loved ones can play after your death,* is what the brochure said. But you couldn't wait for death. We watched you playing the buffoon before the camera and then at the end removing the wig and looking directly at us, serious, handsome. Laugh, you said, this is supposed to be funny.

This was the night you decreed that costumes would be worn at the dinner table. For me, a Hawaiian sarong and a gardenia placed behind my left ear, meaning I was taken. For you, a driving outfit circa 1935—tweed cap, long white scarf, goggles strapped to your forehead. The four boys wore bruises (various shades of green eyeshadow), two of them had black eyes, two wore bloodied bandages wound around their heads. They were having trouble adjusting to their new family. A bit of psychology in appropriate places never hurt, you said, let them trying dressing up in their pain, see if that makes it disappear. The oldest boy—yours, a teenager—had shaved his head and sat in a large high chair asking for his bottle of apple juice, his square of soft blanket. As he sucked the bottle, his blue eyes glazed over—the peaceful journey into sleep had begun. You excused the other three from the table because their weeping was disturbing our conversation.

We were discussing the world and the ways in which it destroys a child's innocence. I'd been reading Bookchin and so at this point was defending the world, arguing that the concept of innocence is outmoded and that it is naïve and dangerous to yearn after an unreflected consciousness. I impressed you by suggesting that the only way to regain innocence is to become brain-damaged—either willingly or by accident. At which point you laughed and said, Bravo! Then, pouring more red wine into my goblet (a French Bordeaux) you toasted the triumph of our love in spite of great obstacles etc. etc., and turned up Nina Simone on the stereo.

The missile once again hovered outside the window. This time we chose to ignore it.

THERE IS A COMPETITION FOR THE HEARTS AND MINDS OF THE PEOPLE

There is a Competition for the Hearts and Minds of the People

I. EARTH

He is calling for an end to the fighting and three days later the government strike heats up and one man was wrestled to the ground. And the cupboard is bare and the union was blamed and we sought to confront the deficit and it could be law within a few days. And we continue to crawl out of the recession and strong growth in the manufacturing sector is forecast and guidelines were laid down and tougher guidelines were laid down in July. And he was not available for comment. And a former justice minister has died and the service sector is suffering. They were stopped by police and their dogs at the border. They are planning to file a complaint and have released their plans. They promise to regain the public interest. A major announcement will come tomorrow and he is keeping his options open and he is convinced he has to do something and no details were released.

2. AIR

He's here to open a trade office and a moderate earthquake shook the city last night and canned goods from supermarket shelves fell onto supermarket aisles. A makeshift morgue has been set up in a football field and the scientists are worried. And the women are worried about take-it-or-leave-it propositions. A delegation was told they should listen to the people but he warns of major stumbling blocks. He says real reasons were sought and key proposals are missing. A major reconstruction program has been set up and a similar plan was put on hold four years ago. He's meeting with the strongest resistance. The women say the process has completely retreated behind closed doors and he says he may not be able to maintain his headquarters and the peacekeepers are nervous. The rescuers are searching through the rubble. A flock of whooping cranes is to be released in Florida next month.

3. FIRE

He still refuses to resign and the protesters have been ordered to disperse. Police will use tear gas if necessary. They're bracing for a bad news budget and thousands have been left homeless. Most of the key suspects avoided capture by committing suicide and the coroner's report is not optimistic. He says he's no fan of the current round of talks, the most critical answers to the most critical questions are still unresolved. Earlier police shot into crowds of protesters. A crowd throwing stones blocked the visit. They fired a warning shot across the bow of the conference. They do not want a confrontation with their giant neighbour. Everyone believes he is behind the violent demonstrations. They say he has psychiatric problems but they don't believe he is dangerous. One of the workers says he fears for his life.

4. WATER

There is a competition for the hearts and minds of the people. It began last week and continues despite stiff opposition. Representatives from the warring factions have been arguing over the plan. The lines are being drawn, the promises given. The proposals are being looked at. He says the victims must take action and a prosperity council is being called for but may be delayed. So far fifty managers from four departments say they'll come to the table. Millions of taxpayers are baffled and the officials insist that there is nothing wrong. More then a million people risk starvation this winter. The party manipulated public fears and now there are concerns. A nicotine by-product has seeped into the nation's drinking supply. And a new rule will be announced tomorrow. He says today's meeting wasn't easy to organize, special deals had to be arranged and he is clearly dissatisfied with the results. There is a void and it needs to be filled. People are dying every day. The ministry says they will look into the matter. There are too many discrepancies in the story. It's possible there are people out there who have information.

Altered Statements

THE DEPARTMENT OF HOPE

If the public has been confused again, we're sorry. We know it happens each morning at daybreak with the unearthing of the Image Store and, like most citizens, we're concerned with the eruption of unsanctioned images which can appear at that time, particularly those images of sickness and death, and of phantom landscapes emitting a strange and haunting beauty. Our early morning radio newscasts which break into sleep have been designed to subvert these rebel images and we urge citizens to make use of them.

We at the Department understand your distress but again remind you that it is dangerous to indulge in independent dreaming and fantasizing or in exotic reading of any kind. Indeed, we actively discourage these seditious practices. Our aim at the Department is the eradication of the unknown and we're confident that the citizenry endorses this goal.

A machine which will program your imagination for you is in the developing stages. In the meantime, continue with your imagination suppressants.

ADDENDUM FROM THE DEPARTMENT OF DEPTH

We realize that the public's impatience with life is due to their lack of success during this season's egg hunt and we take full responsibility for the hunt's failure. Many citizens have complained that the eggs were not only too cleverly hidden but were disguised as well, and therefore we regret the confusion that the giant babies caused. The eggs, of course, were hidden in the babies' fists. But because the babies were hideous, deformed, and mindless, as well as giant, the public refused to approach them. We apologize for the distress and the deaths that subsequently occurred—the public wailing, the suicide epidemic. The giant babies, we believed, were a clever foil for the eggs, and we'd hoped that the public would be more enterprising in searching them out. We know that many citizens feel that something important has been left out of their lives and consequently devote much time and frenzy to the egg hunts in order to recover what they believe they have lost. It is regrettable that this season so few eggs were discovered; each egg contained a drop of wisdom in the form of a printed message imbedded in hexagonal prisms on the egg's surface. The failure of this season's egg hunt has left the public's imagination in a dangerous state of flux.

In order to calm widespread agitation, several of our staff will be on the road during the month of March. As a gesture of goodwill, the Department has initiated a replacement search, one which should not be too difficult for the public to grasp and which offers citizens an opportunity for levity.

Workers will be appearing incognito at public gatherings and the Department is pleased to issue two clues as to their identities:

Clue #1. They will be alone, aloof, and bemused, indicating by their manner an overwhelming lack of need.

Clue #2. During the course of conversation they will be imparting three new insights.

The job of each citizen is, first, to identify the field worker and then engage him or her in conversation during which time the insights will be revealed in full. The three insights are about death, bagpipe music, and balding men, and will be imparted in a lively and amusing manner. We are confident that these new insights will create in each citizen a feeling of joy.

A caution, however. The joy will be temporary, lasting only until the Department's next event, the annual giraffe sightings, when the public's mood will change to one of awe. Already several hundred giraffes are being groomed for the event, their long necks craning above their enclosures in anticipation of the sweet geranium plants which many citizens shyly place for them on their apartment balconies.

PAPER

That's right, Ma'am, we have only one piece of paper left and when we get another one we'll let you know. In the meantime you'll have to try working with empty spaces. There's much to be done with those. No, we don't know when to expect a second piece, these things aren't subject to any known predictions. Paper arrives when it will but we have our people working on it. The last paper storm was some years ago, on the Prairies, but because of the rush, much of it was ripped. And you know we can't predict the storms. As for free paper, it flutters from the heavens at odd occurrences, so there's no predicting that, either. Why don't you try sitting under an oak tree at full moon and see what happens? It could be some time before we get another piece in. Yes, we know it's difficult; our people suggest you try silence instead. Or if you're desperate, what about the margins of old books? Many have tried pasting margins together with some success although we agree it's not the same because of the flaking. Yes, we're sure you've used up your allotment of cardboard boxes but that's no reason to start crying. What about walls? Many are doing that now. The series of novel houses, each room a chapter. It's brought a revival of reader participation for those so inclined. Yes, we realize the electronic screen is useless, there's no taking it to bed and, no, you can't have this last piece of paper. Something of importance might have to be said. In the meantime, take a number and wait in line.

EXPERIMENTS

The practice of putting old people inside metal cages and placing them in schoolyards is to be discouraged. There is not one shred of evidence to support the view that this activity will retard the aging process. Our experiments with caged old people have shown that it is not possible to infuse youth; youth is not a scent that can be worn to dissolve the years. And hundreds of children swarming over such a cage, we have observed, will not result in suppleness in an old person's skin. If anything, under such conditions, old people become even more cranky than they already are; it has been reported that a number of children have been scratched by the elderly trying to grab their arms and legs through the bars. Side-effects from the caging of old people: namely, they rapidly turn a dull yellow colour—both skin and clothing—which is most unpleasant to view; they become adept at issuing profanities, delivered at the shriller end of the musical scale; and if left unattended for longer than two weeks, they turn into granite, a stone of little use to the industrial world.

Our experiments further indicate that the youth of children cannot be extracted, rubbed off, or otherwise worn with positive results by an old person. Practices such as jumping from schoolyard roofs into groups of children, smothering oneself with children at birthday parties, rolling with them under Christmas trees, or the wearing of small children on the back like a bulky shawl are of little use, as is the practice of maintaining a child-like demeanour. For these reasons, the Department of Experiments strongly suggests that old people abandon the pursuit of joy and return to their small airless rooms. We find it distressing to witness their mindless capering on the public lawns—old men riding tricycles, old women dancing with each other in wedding dresses. The public lawns should be left to the solemn pursuit of childhood play.

URGENT MISSIVE CONCERNING THE BORING WHITE WOMAN LOBBY

Even though it is the stated mandate of this Department to integrate minority groups into mainstream culture whenever and wherever possible, the Department is still not willing to entertain the demands from the Boring White Woman lobby. We are not yet convinced that they constitute a minority in the classic sense, despite their repeated attempts to convince us otherwise—the petitions, demonstrations, media events, and so forth. Events, we might add, which can only be described as exercises in pitiless whining. Furthermore, the Department rejects their claim that they constitute a minority group because they live—happily, they insist—with men. Attendance on children is also not proof of visible minority status and no amount of Mother's Day cards delivered to this office in black plastic bags will persuade us otherwise. Motherhood has been known to cross all boundaries, both of gender and colour, and is not the special domain of Boring White Women. In fact, we expect a public apology from the Boring White Woman lobby because of their challenge to our declaration that the old-style nuclear family is dead; we expect nothing less than their denouncing of this abhorrent fantasy.

The aim of this department is the disbanding of the Boring White Woman lobby into more appropriate groupings—into one of the many victim groups, perhaps, or into associations for the specifically afflicted.

Staff are again reminded that fraternizing with Boring White Women will not be tolerated, and any Department member who attends a Boring White Woman event as a guest will be immediately dismissed. (Refer to the enclosed invitation, THE BORING WHITE WOMAN REVUE.) Such invitations are never harmless; Boring White Women are legend for their guile and deviously feminine ways while maintaining an outer appearance of shallowness. In truth, they are extremists and their attempts to gain minority status is an infiltration tactic, a ploy to regain their formerly privileged position.

The influence of the Boring White Woman lobby must be countered at every turn; they've had enough special attention and their access to special programmes for minority groups will continue to be denied. Do not believe the Boring White Woman lobby when they claim they are lesbians, if not in body, then at least in heart.

Effective immediately there will be a ban on Boring White Woman charity events. The Department of Diversity declares that citizens will no longer be won over by the obvious sentiment of such endeavours. Diseases and the Poor will now be championed by one of the minority groups from our approved list, crushing once and for all, we believe, the irritatingly benevolent social worker image for which the

Boring White Woman is renowned. As well, the following bans continue: bridge groups; committee work; self-help groups which focus on maintaining loving relationships with men; and mindless consumerism which, we now know, is the special province of Boring White Woman.

Field workers are urged to continue in their derision of the Boring White Woman lobby, keeping in mind our recent and spectacular successes in dealing with their counterpart, The Dead White Male, now reduced to whimpering on the sidelines of history.

In closing, congratulations are due to those staff members who have successfully forayed into Boring White Woman territory—the suburbs. The Department is pleased to note that several of our favourite special interest groups are now operating within the public schools where they have wrested control of the parent-teacher agendas. It is cheering to see the Boring White Women lobby marginalized to the status of hot dog server where they belong. May they remain there.

DISASTERS

Field report: five households surveyed.

Household #1: All the disasters were pretty good but we liked the earthquake the best because of the way the freeway bridge snapped in half like it was a pretzel. We liked seeing the survivors and rescuers tell their stories; they looked so beautiful on TV, so solemn and eloquent. Some even cried and we liked that; we appreciated the way the camera got up close to their faces, catching their tears in mid-flow.

Household #2: Watching the volcano erupt and the lava flow in its slow, deadly path towards the subdivision was pretty upsetting for everyone and we were glad there was a panel discussion after the show because our fears were erupting all over the living room and we needed reassurance. Volcano experts said eruptions only occur where there's a volcano, so we're glad we live on the flatlands; no lava's ever going to squish our house even though it looked nice in the TV picture, cracked grey and hot pink inside, quite lovely. What we have to worry about here is snakes and poisonous spiders and you should have a disaster show about them, the way the victims die and all that.

Household #3: We hated the hurricane; it was so boring. No rooftops flying, no cars flipping over. You do see a couple of black kids crouched beneath a freeway overpass and a lot of severely blown glass but so what? The only interesting thing was the way the hurricane dwarfed ordinary ranchers but we only got to see that for a couple of seconds. On the whole don't bother with hurricanes again. Not unless we get to see some real destruction, squashed bodies and a lot of blood. We give the hurricane a 2.

Household #4: The flash flood made everyone mad. Because it served them right. There they were, a guy and a woman and her six-year-old daughter sitting on the roof of a pickup truck, stranded in the middle of a muddy, fast-flowing river. They shouldn't have been there in the first place, any idiot could see that. That guy was stupid (stupid!) to drive across the river. Several residents of the area even said as much. In future, if you're going to have a flash flood you'd better warn people not to drive through it. Watching that guy and woman and kid on top of the pickup for so long was really irritating. We could imagine the argument they were probably having because the guy figured he could make it and didn't. And not the kid's father, either, that was obvious—baseball cap, fat, and a beer drinker to boot, a low-life is what we figured. When the helicopter finally came our hearts went out to the Grandmother waiting on the shore with a blanket for the kid. Everyone here hopes she'll get custody because it's plain the mother has no sense when it comes to men; her choice nearly cost the kid her life.

Household #5: We think the Department should beef up its disaster series; this month's offerings were ordinary fare and we're getting bored with the show. The freak wave was a bust: an old woman toppled like a stick doll, a screaming ambulance, cars smashing against each other, a baby howling inside a semi-floating station wagon. Big deal. In our opinion, the Department needs to have death make an actual appearance. There needs to be bleeding bodies and hysterical, mourning mothers hurling themselves over the corpses. The closest the Department came to real-life disaster was during the earthquake: a car, a new Accura Integra, squashed under the freeway. The car was only eighteen inches high; the fireman said the car didn't have a chance. Now, that's a disaster!

Please add your suggestions to the preceding list keeping

in mind that all disasters must be "natural"; i.e. not subject to political interference and not environmentally sensitive. Forthcoming disasters will focus on "killer" insects and reptiles, collapsing mountains—mudslides, avalanches, rockslides and the like—and freak windstorms, with an emphasis on toppling powerlines and the spectacular profusion of life- threatening electrical sparks which can occur at these times.

SCAPE

WE ARE THE AMORPHOUS AUDIENCE NERVOUS FOR ANOTHER FUNFIX. WE DO NOT INTERACT, WE BEHOLD; WE VIEW, ARE TARGETED AS AUDIENCE, AS VIEWERS. WE ENGAGE AND DISENGAGE LIKE MOTORS. WE CLAP LIKE MORONS BEFORE SELECTED FUNNYMEN. THE FUNNY WOMEN ARE ALL UGLY. WE DISH IT UP; WE LIKE IT TASTELESS. WE COLOUR CO-ORDINATE OUR IDEAS TO MATCH THE PREVAILING WINDS, THIS YEAR NEON, NEXT YEAR RUST. THE ONLY RELIEF OCCURS WHEN FEAR BREAKS THROUGH THE FIFTEEN ALLOWABLE SHADES OF PLEASURE TO PANIC THE VIEWING HERDS OVER TV CLIFFS. WE'VE BECOME NO MORE THAN A CHIP OF AN HISTORICAL SOUND BYTE. NO MORE THAN EARLY BIRDS SHOPPING FOR THE ENDLESS BIRTH AND REBIRTH OF CELEBRITIES. THERE IS NO ESCAPING THE MARKET RESEARCHERS. WE ARE PIGEONS WITH A STARRING ROLE IN A VIDEO CALLED "TARGET PRACTICE." WE ARE BEING TAPED BEFORE A DEAD AUDIENCE. TOMORROW IS A POP SONG.

SECRETS

AN IMPORTANT NOTICE TO ALL ENFORCEMENT OFFICERS

The terrorist group SPEIV (Society to Prevent the Eradication of Inner Voices) has resurfaced. Printed messages have been appearing randomly on citizens' home entertainment screens, on several of the giant television terminals which line the major freeways, and on work screens at the Department of Silence. Public exposure has been limited because the duration of these messages has been brief and, to date, the public's distress level remains low. This, of course, could change in a matter of hours, erupting into the hysteria and gruesome public flagellations that occurred during previous SPEIV assaults. Officers should therefore be warned that a major SPEIV offensive may be in the offing. The following captured fragment may indicate the direction such an assault might take. It is reproduced and circulated under conditions of strict secrecy and will be the subject of the next departmental meeting. Department members may wish to take a reaction suppressant before reading it.

" *. . . the Department of Secrets says there are no secrets. But we say there are many secrets. Here are some of them:*

1. *The idea of the unknown has been obliterated; what's palpable has been made unknowable enough.*
2. *Your consciousness has been willingly limited; any 'other' reality is now classified as mental illness.*
3. *Your consciousness has fled; your consciousness is in hiding.*
4. *The subversive wing of SPEIV operates under the name "The Rules*

& Regulations of an Institute called Tranquility" in celebration of our spiritual mentor, William Hone (circa 1807), the great English satirist who pioneered the role of the public informer. Who throughout his works said, "conscience makes cowards of us all." Who dared to ridicule royalty, self-serving governments and all oppressors of vibrant, questioning thought. We are proud to call ourselves Honers, to sharpen our wit, to perform our random assaults in his honour. To gather together voicing our rallying cry: EVERYTHING MUST BE QUESTIONED. *We dedicate ourselves to splendour and diversity. We are the protectors of the unforeseen, the perpetuators and guardians of the novel. Join us. Imagine a strange singing, a mechanical choir erupting from the cities like the whistles and clanking of broken pipes. It is still possible for our silenced voices to be heard. . . .*

THE WORK

The Work

I'd been busy on the edge all day, sweeping up the dust, hanging up a few stray thoughts. People kept calling me in but I lingered because the air was so still, the ground so smooth, and it was difficult to leave. I wasn't that far away, just at the edge of the garden, but it seemed a distance.

Looking up at the house, the windows were filled with children calling my name. "Come in, come in," they cried, "haven't you been out there long enough? And we're hungry, there's nothing to eat."

Even the old ones were at the windows calling. "It's not for us," they yelled, "it's for you. You'll catch your death standing in drafty doorways like that."

"I'll catch my death anyway," I yelled back, "sooner than later."

"Don't talk ridiculous," the old ones said, shaking their heads. "You're not meant to turn your back on the world."

Instructions for My Daughter

Watch out for tall men in black suits playing soccer in the school field for insurance salesmen dressed in vestments for solitary men with teddy bears propped in the backseats of cars never lower your eyes but keep watching for the times of loss all around you girls are being stolen they won't believe the danger they didn't watch out for knives glinting in the sun's rays for large boats with few passengers for promises of dresses the colour of sapphire for tea parties that only drunks attend so keep watching watch out for the heat of bones tearing against naked flesh for the heat of blood invisible like red satin beneath a black velvet gown for the stench of fried feelings meaning love's gone dead for the bloat of boredom never lower your eyes because the world's injustice occurs one spoonful at a time to wear you down because the world will never believe the story how the saints flaked and fell from empty towers how TV screens replaced the glory how some cried out but their crying was swallowed by engine noise how there are many amongst us who are battered by neglect and dread and how they want to tell us things keep watching never lower your eyes because you must confront these people listen to what they have to say there's danger they'll tell you there's danger everywhere

Rules

As usual we were talking about kids, this time what to do when one of them brings home a stray story, one you don't want kept around the house, one you don't want texturing their lives. For example the story my daughter told about the afternoon she spent with her friend and her friend's baby-sitter watching a video on TV, *The Addams Family*. Then afterwards how they hung around talking, two eleven-year-old girls and this twenty-year-old babysitter named Crystal.

Naturally I wanted to know what they talked about and this is what my daughter said: Men, we talked about men. How you should never live with your boyfriend. Crystal's lived with five of them and they all got crazy on her. So she told us not to bother living with guys and I believe that; Crystal's been around and knows what she's saying.

All right, I said, I'll go along with that.

But my daughter talked some more, this time about witches. She said: Crystal wears a long black wig because it looks better for being a witch in. She's got these three girlfriends and they're all going to live together and be witches and she's going to plant marigolds around the house to keep out evil forces. One time Crystal even talked to Marilyn Monroe on the Ouija board, it's true. Marilyn Monroe told Crystal she was really murdered, how three men came into her bedroom carrying hammers and made her swallow a bunch of pills. Marilyn Monroe's that dead movie star, right? Well, Marilyn Monroe told Crystal she should believe everything she reads in the *National Enquirer*. And she told Crystal this: Don't live with a man 'til you're over thirty because they treat you like idiots before that. So that's why Crystal's going to be a witch. She's through with men 'til she turns thirty. She says she can do a lot of good being a witch, she's got ten years to practice, and she can do things like making the wheat grow and finding a cure for herpes and getting even with those five guys that went crazy on her just like they did on *The Addams Family*, turn them into toads and things.

In discussing this story of men, witches, and Ouija boards we decided that the best response is no response, the bored uh-huh-isn't-that-interesting-change-the-subject response. Adding three more rules to all the rest: one, keep your mouth shut; two, control your impulse to go berserk; and three, believe your power as a parent is always greater than that of an apprentice-witch.

Repeat these rules like a mantra. That is, unless you want a stray story to become an important part of your kid's life, somehow remembered as a kind of collosal turning point, as in: so that was when I came to love the putrid underbelly of things.

Cats in Toronto

There were four of them plus the mother and the mother's sister all locked in the laundry room downstairs, mewing and messing on the floor. The place stank so much we hated to use the washer and dryer. But it wasn't up to us to handle the problem because we believe it's bad manners to clean up someone else's cat shit. We believe it's up to the person who owns the cats, in this case the girl who'd left her boyfriend the week before and moved back home. But was hardly there. She'd left water and a bowl of crunchies in the laundry room but ignored the litter box; it had spilled all over the floor.

We were staying on vacation at her parents' house, the parents away in Florida. Escaping the city, they said, because sometimes Toronto sucks the big one. And weren't we lucky, we figured, a place to stay for free but should have known a hitch would occur, somehow you always pay. In this case with cat shit fumes, there's this horrible smell and no one is doing anything about it, particularly not the girl. She's twenty-three, a newly grown-up person. We figured she should know about proper cat shit etiquette. We figured her parents would have told her all about that. We would have even forgiven her ignorance had she stuck around for a meal with us, maybe carted out one load of shit instead of going to pool parties or crying in her friend's car parked outside. Crying about the boyfriend not loving her anymore when she loved him so so much.

The kittens were cute, white and grey; we figured she'd have had no trouble finding them homes at the SPCA. Our kids spent hours playing with them on the back lawn, had names for them like Tish, Ginger, Spunk, and Puffy, and regularly begged us to take them home (two thousand miles to Vancouver via Fiesta West). They couldn't care less about broken hearts.

So there we were trapped on vacation at her parents' house, using the pool, sleeping in the king-size bed, breathing in all those cat shit fumes, but stalling about breaking an important rule of etiquette, putting it off, waiting around like dumb bunnies for her parents to return. We figured they should be the ones to tell her: *Do something with these cats or they're going to the pound.* That always gets things moving.

The Date

Because we believe that when you marry a man *he* marries your family, we make it a practice to attend our daughter's dates. Might as well see what's in store for everyone *now*, we reason. So far, our three teenaged daughters haven't objected to this practice—in fact, it's kept dating to a minimum. They only ask that when they *do* go on dates, we stay in the background, that is, sit in the *back* seat of the car or let *them* sit next to the date in the movies.

The last date we went on was Reta's, our oldest, a nineteen-year-old beauty with an alarming eye for older men. In this case, Harvey Troutman, a middle-aged building contractor, small, muscular, moustached, living in a ground-floor apartment, sparsely furnished but neat and clean. An older man to be sure, set in his ways, no doubt, but secure financially; a man who's made his way in the world erecting condominiums.

For the date I took along the family dog and the fornication kit containing, among other things, Sexual Body Paint and ocean wave music. I have found that openly displaying this kit which is large, black, and labelled—actually one of Father's tackleboxes—can have a deterring effect on the romantic aspirations of the date in question. To my knowledge the kit has yet to be used.

Harvey Troutman was a little surprised when Reta arrived with an entourage for his cozy candlelit dinner at home. But he graciously invited us in. I will say that, initially, we made the dog lay outside the window where he could watch us.

The dinner party, it seemed, had a nautical theme; Harvey Troutman was wearing a white sailor's hat, one of those round ones that children wear for tap dance routines in Spring reviews. He gave Reta a hat, apologizing to me that he only had two on hand. I told him that if we'd known about the hats, I could have brought my own; we keep a supply of these hats in the hall closet for occasions such as this.

Harvey Troutman looked askance, saying, Ahhh! and began serving the drinks: for Reta, wine and overproof rum over ice; for me, warm beer.

Did I mention that we brought Grandma along? She wasn't in that apartment five minutes before she'd picked apart Harvey Troutman's floral centrepiece of lavender and delphinium, adding to it some of the rocks and gravel she'd brought in with her, concealed inside her black rubber boots. (She does this because she has a fear of floating—the rocks and gravel keep her anchored to the ground.) When the flower arrangement was to her liking, she placed it on the floor beside the coffee table. Plainly perturbed, Harvey Troutman said through his teeth, Please leave it alone. (We noticed, then, that his dentures were straight and white.) But Grandma only said, Nonsense, I have lavender at home much bigger than yours.

After this, Harvey Troutman sighed and moved onto the couch beside Reta. He put his arm around her shoulder, trying to make small talk by asking her what kind of music she liked best. Oh, Reta said, I don't know, just everything, but never rock and roll in the daytime. Harvey Troutman seemed pleased to hear this, pointing out to her his new music technology, a sinister little silver and black unit displayed against the bare wall.

But sitting on that couch before the meal we did feel sorry for the poor dog watching us from outside on the bit of lawn, especially when it began to rain. It was too much for Grandma, she had to let him in, opening the sliding glass door. The dog was overjoyed and, muddy paws and all, bounded into the room. My daughter said, Here baby, and the grateful dog climbed onto her lap.

Then knock, knock. An uninvited neighbour said she'd love to join us for dinner. An overbearing woman, introducing herself as Darlene. It was soon plain that this woman wanted Harvey Troutman for herself. I knew this for sure when Darlene took me aside in the kitchen and said, Harvey Troutman's not a faithful man, you wouldn't believe the string of women in and out of this place, a regular daisy chain!

Dinner was served in a tiny alcove off the kitchen. At table

Harvey Troutman called me *Mother*, though we're the same age, and asked me if I'd make the sauce for the hamburgers. Just mix some ketchup with lemon juice, he said.

Fish sauce with hamburgers? Grandma snorted, scandalized. Never heard of it!

But, in order to keep my presence as innocuous as possible, as is the agreement with our daughters, I mixed the sauce. And, of course, it went all wrong, becoming like soup, running over the hamburgers and soaking through the buns.

It was then I started laughing and couldn't stop. Reta, who'd seemed bored with the date up to this point and was playing with the lettuce and tomato on her plate, gave me a wan smile. And Grandma laughed too, shaking her head, and wheezing with her eyes shut tight in that peculiar way she has.

I looked at Harvey Troutman who'd pinched his lips together, looking displeased. At this moment, I made up our minds: Clearly we're not marrying a man who doesn't have a sense of humour.

Kristmas Kraft

I heard about this cute Christmas gift idea that you can make at home—your own Kraft nativity scene, colourful too, and mmmmm yummy.

First, hollow out a three-pound brick of your favourite luncheon meat so that it resembles a stable and so that you, looking down through its roof, look like an angel. Then put your stable onto a cookie sheet and surround it with shredded coconut. This is the hay. Next, stick four toothpicks into four wieners and stand them up. Top each wiener with a Kraft green olive. These are the cattle. For Mary, top an upright cocktail wiener with a Mini-Mallow and use strands of coconut for her hair. A hollowed-out Maxi-Mallow will do for the manger, and the infant Jesus will be a cocktail wiener wrapped in a Kraft cheese single. Surround the table and the hay with Miracle Whip and shredded Velveeta Cheese.

Take a picture.

Then place your Kraft nativity scene in a three hundred and seventy-five degree oven for forty-five minutes. Serve when friends drop over on Boxing Day or use as a festive centrepiece, a Merry Christmas gift from Mom in the kitchen, that happy lady, that wise shopper.

Oven

Jungly the word kept coming up in her notebook part of a spelling bee but then pictures of a chimpanzee playing scrabble at the kitchen table as well and a grey cat laying on the front porch mat chewing a bone and children swinging through the trees her children and there were many of them these things were all in the notebook and in the midst of this while the jungle swirled around her she lay ill on the floor just managing to whisper in a small raw voice spell denude spell reckless spell escape

Over at my noteboook that grey cat again chewing a bone on the front porch stairs and dawn pounding in on huge cat feet with meat in its teeth this time yes yes an enormous carnivore come to devour the day and children flinging themselves out of windows doors barefooting it across morning grass past parked cars slimy with dew and she and I busy at the kitchen counter baking poems just she and I and the words between us trays upon trays still warm from the oven one for you one for you one for you

Broccoli

At the Pensioners' Thanksgiving turkey dinner we were sitting sedately around a traditional English table mildly eating our meal when a dump truck backed into the dining hall and right up to our table in fact right across from my plate it had a load of steamed broccoli pale green in that wilted English way and it dumped the entire lot onto my plate none of the other diners even seemed to notice but carried blandly on with their meals first turkey then a forkful of mashed potatoes all pushed around in the beige gravy meanwhile how to tackle this enormous pile of broccoli where to begin? you could see the meanwhiles everywhere bald heads pearled necks and no one noticing the sudden hill of broccoli pale green and steaming right there on my plate in fact almost blocking my view of the other diners eating their turkey but not broccoli no one else had broccoli everyone else had peas they were nodding serenely before their peas turkey potatoes gravy eyes half lidded you could tell they were giving thanks you could see it in their mild soft faces all this broccoli did not exist for them no broccoli laden dump trucks backed onto their calm English dinner plates ever there was nothing left to do but ask for butter pass the butter please there was nothing left to do at the Pensioners' Thanksgiving turkey dinner but take the frontal approach and spear the hill of broccoli salt pepper butter first one mouthful thankfully eaten then another

Spin a Bible

Let your fingers land where it says tiny high-rise kitchens where it says chrome so clean an angel might mistake its pristine shine for an enchanted lake and fall through where it says there are grease stains in our sink a guide for our conducted tour where it says we mustn't grumble mustn't fuss there are fools all around to make us laugh they will have us ringing with reasons where it says shake of the dice everything nice such a pleasant journey interlude trip squawk sing that's the thing just jabbering songbirds 'til our short days are done where it says we're mad all mad the meaning we give all in a stream sucked down the drain

Ownership

I found the woman with tatoos on her arm who'd stolen my daughter. She'd chained her to the TV set in a tiny downtown apartment. Left her all day with pop and chips and *Archie* comics but didn't harm her in any way. Just said she wanted someone to come home to. Just said she wanted someone to live for.

My life: one long lonely trail, she said.

So I offered to share my daughter with her. Look, I said, you can visit on Sundays, be like a favourite aunt, come to all the occasions—Christmas, birthdays, Mother's Day, Easter.

No, the woman said, I want to come home to the girl myself every night after slaving at the factory.

So I said: You can rent the downstairs room at our house,

come home to us all—me, my daughter, my sons, the dog, the husband—we all need someone to come home to.

But the woman was being unreasonable. You can't have her, she said, I want her, having in mind pink ribbons for her hair, I'm planning to call her Daisy.

So I felt bad, then, because this meant the woman was crazy, a danger, and I'd have to get tough, call in the cops, an army of neighbours, saw the chains off my daughter, have the woman arrested. If only she'd been reasonable we could have shared my girl. Who wanted to get home in the worst way, see her cat, and put her own life back onto its proper channel.

ATTIC

Attic

We kept the baby hidden in the attic. He grew to adolescence up there, still hidden.

Yes, we knew the war was long over, that there was, in fact, no war at all. But the random gangs, we knew about those, the gangs looking for converts.

And we didn't want our son taken from us. He was better hidden than a rat.

You hear of these things.

Frightened people shuttered away. Coming out only at night, in the dark, for food and exercise. During any war there are people hidden like this; it's not unusual to stay hidden for years.

Only now there is no war. Not like we knew it. We don't have to be told this; we went to school, we still read books. The idea of war has changed, the threat has become non-specific and everywhere like smoke—vague, difficult to name.

We've kept our son hidden these many years, afraid to show him to the world. A few children have to remain untainted or what of the future?

We go about our daily lives: we buy food, we work in airless rooms. The world thinks we are childless. But we have our son in the attic. Like a private faith, a secret knowing. The neighbours may regard us with pity but they needn't bother; we have achieved transcendence.

Now and then you hear of these things.

On Holiday with Giants

FOR TERRY

Our children are larger than us. They carry us about on their huge backs like packsacks, you on the boy, me on the girl. Riding them through the city streets in search of playmates it's evident that other parents are being carried about in a similar way; some are even slung on their children's hips like bags of groceries, some ride anxiously on fat shoulders. Then we are set down in designated areas for drink and conversation, dozens of parents gathered together for worried viewing of the park across the way; the children are playing their fearsome games there with baseballs the size of pumpkins, and bats sturdy enough to support a house. Grandparents, no bigger than dolls, sit amongst us nodding quietly to one another: Ah, the wisdom of the world!

At night it's back to the hotel room. You and I in a corner

sharing a mattress on the floor. The children each with a king- sized bed arranged before the TV set where they watch game shows and eat peanuts—the shells rising in mountains from the floor. The room growing smaller by the minute. The children growing larger and larger.

During the night the room heats up like an incubator. But the children don't notice. They sleep with massive fists thrust in their pink gaping mouths. When our daughter laughs and tosses in her sleep her roundness bruises the hotel walls. At three a.m. our son cries out in a man's voice: Barricade the door, the troops are coming! His size-twelve feet flailing against the hotel quilt.

We, on the floor, sweat and lose moisture, shrivel a little more, dry out. Our lotions of little help. Our lovemaking of little help. We keep reducing in volume. Peanut shells spill onto our mattress. On the way to the bathroom we wade through a clutter of pop cans and pizza cartons, track shoes, comics.

Regarding these sleeping giants, we realize it's too late not to have had them. The die has been cast. Inexplicably, our pride in them remains.

Big

It goes like this: guy comes to the club, drives up in a Corvette convertible. We're out on the street waiting for him. Okay, it's not cool hanging out there but here's the exception: this guy's a celebrity and we want to see how he handles the car. We want to see the car. Because the car's famous, too. There's as many pictures of it in the magazines as there is of him. The guy used to be Mr. California; the car was his prize when he won. And it don't disappoint. But Mr. California does. Looking nothing like his pictures. Looking about half of what he was in his pictures.

"Put her there," he says, sticking out his hand and I grab it first. An all right shake, but you'd expect more from a former Mr. California. You'd expect it to hurt or something.

I haven't been at the club long, five months maybe, but

in that time I've gone from one sixty to one eighty-five. Lance, the trainer, says I'm doing good; in another year, who knows, maybe the Regionals. I've still got things to work on: abs, pecs, thighs, and I've got to get over feeling weird about being greased up and posing in front of crowds. But Lance says it'll come. He says, "Posing is an art form, not everyone's got the style, but you, you just might have it."

Mr. California's come to give a talk. Give a scare, is more like it.

Afterwards, when I get home, this is what I hear: "Mini's been barking at your door all afternoon. It's been driving me nuts."

It's my Mom talking. She's sitting at the kitchen table, her usual place, working on the crossword. Even though it's June, the windows are shut, the blinds are pulled. The overhead light is switched on. She says she feels cooler in the dark. "Don't ask me why," she says, "but darkness and coolness go together; it's something to do with the mind."

I can't stand the heat inside the house; I open the back door and the front door. Something like a wind starts up; the curtains blow, the crossword starts flapping under my Mom's hand. "Jesus, Wade." This is the sum total of what she says and does. Wind banging against her stiff blonde hair.

Mini's still barking outside my bedroom door. She hardly pays attention when I bend down to pat her hello. Inside the room Melissa's restless, shoving her body against the cage. When she does this, Mini always barks to let me know it's feeding time at the zoo.

The thing I like about Mini is how she guards my room, won't even let my Mom get near. Pitbulls are like that; they pick themselves a job and that's the only thing they'll do. Fetch a stick? Go for a walk? Forget it.

I make a visit to Death Row in the basement. There's three cages down there, side by side; one for the mothers and their young, one for the teenagers, one for the grown-ups big enough to become dinner. They're brown rats with tiny black eyes and they squeal when they're put in the cage with Melissa. A boa constrictor eats a rat a week. First they squeeze them to death, then they eat them whole. As soon as Melissa smells the rat she starts licking the air. I always picture Melissa smiling at me and saying thanks when I drop a live rat in her cage.

While Melissa's having her dinner, Mini stands by the cage watching and wagging her tail. You'd think she'd just been given a meaty bone. She's that happy.

Mr. California looked like an ordinary guy. Meaning his body wasn't that great. His upper looked puny and there wasn't much left of the biceps. Weighing about one ninety. While he was talking to us, I had to keep remembering this: he *used to be* Mr. California. *Used to be. Used to be.*

He sat on Lance's desk at the back of the gym. He had on a white T-shirt with a collar and dark blue slacks; he looked more like a golfer. There were about ten of us listening to his talk. Which was about why we shouldn't use steroids. It was like the talks we got in school: a former drug addict, some wrecked guy, telling us to stay off drugs; a former gang member showing us his scars from the bullets, telling us to clean up our act or we'll end up as corpses. And here's a former champion telling us about steroids. Ask me a question: Where have all the formers gone? And I'll tell you this: they're standing in front of a bunch of dummies telling them not to do what they did.

Mr. California started out slow. Started out praising the sport. He said he could tell we were all in great shape. He said bodybuilding is about getting big, getting huge, it's about getting your body fat down to a lean, mean percentage. He said, "I believe bodybuilders are the most dedicated athletes on the planet." He talked like it was over for him. "I loved every aspect of the sport," he said, " but most of all I enjoyed getting big. I've always been known as the guy with the biggest legs in bodybuilding. How big were they? At my peak, believe it or not, they measured a massive thirty-two inches each!"

"Wow," we all said.

Mr. California said two years ago when he won the title he was twenty-five years old and weighed three hundred pounds. "I'd shot up so many steroids I couldn't fit in the Corvette," he said. "I had to get my girlfriend to drive it home."

Back in the kitchen I start loading up. First a tin of Mus-L-Blast protein drink. Then two steaks, fried rare. With a loaf of bread and two litres of homo.

My Mom says, "You give that snake another Shirley?"

"Yeah," I says.

My Mom smiles. She calls every rat Shirley. Ever since Dad moved in with that cocktail waitress by the same name.

On the fridge door I've posted the creed of the Iron Men:

1. Train heavy
2. Never miss workouts
3. Take every workout like it's your last
4. Set impossible goals (and make them happen)
5. The means justify the end
6. THINK BIG

While I'm eating my Mom starts yapping: "When are you going to get a job, Wade?"

I try not to listen.

"When are you going to start paying for all this food? And the money for the club? I'm only working part-time and your Dad gives me nothing. Wade, answer me. If you're not going back to school what are you going to do?"

But what I'm thinking is this: if I add a fourth set of bench presses to my workout maybe I can speed up things in the thigh department. And I'm thinking this: The ad for Boron says: "Increase your testosterone levels by 300 percent." It says, "Higher testosterone means faster, easier muscle growth."

The thing the guys wanted to know from Mr. California was about drug tests. If he took so many steroids, how come he didn't get caught? Don't they have urine tests to check a guy out?

"Sure," Mr. California said, "but this is what I'd do. I'd get a friend to piss in a jar for me, then I'd put my friend's piss in a syringe and inject it into my own bladder. That way when it came time for the test, I'd be giving them someone else's piss. A Mr. World contender told me how to do that."

I like the idea about thinking big. I was thinking big when I got Melissa. I was thinking no one else I know has a boa constrictor for a pet. We got along right away. I took to wearing her around my neck; I liked the weight of her, the feel. And the way the women, who come to play cards with my Mom on Tuesday nights, would cringe and pull away. I'd go up to them with Melissa, saying, "She's really friendly, she won't hurt you. If you stroke her head, she'll lick your hand."

The other thing was the rats. I'd say, "Come on, I'll show you downstairs, the way everything's set up like an assembly line."

I liked hearing my Mom tell them: "He's really done a clever job. It's amazing the way it works. But I've got to warn you about the smell. Take a deep breath. The smell can knock you dead."

When we're alone I try to get my Mom to wear Melissa. "Keep that thing away from me," she yells, and leaves the room.

Mr. California told about starting out. "I looked like a

track team geek," he said, "skinny, with wide hips and narrow shoulders. That didn't stop me, though. My driving ambition was to get as freaked-out big as humanly possible, and I proved beyond a shadow of a doubt that even a guy with lousy genetics like mine could do just that. Hell, I was so huge, my back looked like a map with mountains and valleys. 'Better not get too close to me,' I'd tell my opponents, 'you're liable to get lost in a crevice.' "

The track team geek part. That was good. Remind me to forget about school.

Then Mr. California said, "But I paid the price, did I ever. Steroids are a killer, guys; you can still reach your goals without using steroids. Hard work and nutrition. That's the secret. Go for the long term. The short term's a bummer."

He's got that right.

The short term.

Dad's been gone six months. He left two days after Christmas. My Mom said, "When he gets sick of that bimbo he'll want to come back home. Home is where the harpy is," she said, "but just let him try."

Shirley's twenty-three, six years older than me. I've seen her two times. Once waiting in the car when Dad stopped by to get his fishing rod. The other time waiting in line to see *Beauty and the Beast.* Grease up my Mom and Shirley and put them on stage, side by side, and there'd be no contest.

That time at the movie, Dad and I pretended we were strangers. There's a way you can look right through a person: you can stare and stare and make them disappear.

A term I'm hearing a lot at the club is "going ballistic." It means getting mad, freaking out, exploding. It's the attitude

Lance says we should use in our training, it's putting fire power in our training. "It takes balls to go ballistic," is what Lance says. It's something my Mom should do. Sitting around in a housecoat is for losers.

Mr. California talked for half an hour before he told us he was a dying man. "I won't live to see thirty," he said, "because I have brain cancer." All because he used steroids. He has a wrecked liver, too, and a few other things wrong with him. But the main thing he had to say was that he is dying.

"The only good thing about being off steroids," he said, "apart from the death sentence, is that my weight's gone down to normal; I can finally fit inside the Corvette."

The Corvette has monster wheels and can do one fifty, no sweat, is what he told us.

A couple of times a week I fill the bathtub about six inches deep and let Melissa slide around in the water. Let her pretend she's back in some South American swamp. She's five and a half feet long and still growing. She's that big and all she eats is rats.

About Mr. California, what I think is this: the means justify the end. Bodybuilding is about setting goals and then achieving them. Mine is to become so big there won't be room in this world for anyone else.

Alice & Stein

That first while Stein carried her bride around Paris in a white canvas bag. I will have the introductions slow, she said, only a few will meet her.

Those fortunate few would join them for dinner in the Louvre where a wooden table had been set up in the foyer beneath Michaelangelo's sculpture of David. Stein would heave the canvas bag onto the table. Inside was tiny Alice Toklas.

My bride, said Stein, my beautiful, beautiful bride, dark and gnarly as a walnut. She lifted Alice Toklas gently by the belly and placed her on a chair.

Don't put me near the window, Alice screamed, you know how I hate a view!

Stein excelled at performing on stage. Any opportunity and she'd build a platform, often with boards and nails. She'd build one anywhere. Showing up at a former friend's house, after years and years, she'd start building a platform in the backyard, hauling the 2x4s herself, adding planks as needed. The friend's children mistaking her for a stranger, this heavyset, short woman with the smooth, tanned skin and the hook nose, her hair cut like a man's, like Caesar's. No, you couldn't call her handsome—intriguing perhaps, a little frightening. But what things she knew! What secrets she told from her stage!

Stein wrote for twenty minutes each day. You can write a lot of books if you do that, she said. She also said: No one cares if you don't write.

But mostly Stein thought: About how to end the nineteenth century. . . . How to pull the world of literature into the twentieth century. . . . How to make a composition of language. . . . How to make words stay on the page composed. . . . Everything I have done has been influenced by Cezanne and Flaubert, she said.

Tramping over the hills and roadways of southern France, wandering through the streets of Paris in search of building materials for her many platforms. Thinking: One human being is as important as another . . . a blade of grass has the same value as a tree . . . in composition, all words have the same value.

One or other of her dogs as companion, her two great Standard Poodles, Basket and Basket 2.

She said: I like a thing simple but it must be simple through complication.

She said: Biography is the true form of the twentieth century.

✧

Things As They Are . . . Potomac . . . The Making of Americans . . .

✧

Alice kept house. Her job: sweeping up the unknown. Not a leisurely sweeping, but a rushed, hurried sweeping. There's only so much time! she'd cry, and so much dust!

The more she swept, the more she uncovered. She swept up bucketfuls of dirt, clumps of mud, dust as plentiful as sand. Once she unearthed an unpublished book of poems by Rimbaud. The first page, first sentence reading: Wants! Those gnarly fingers from Hell!

Stein dismissed the book saying: Too much passion, too many birds flying off the page.

✧

One time Stein roped together some logs in a harbour, then climbed aboard. Another platform. This was in Marseilles. When no one paid attention, she suspended a cable 100 feet from a bridge, attached the cable to the back of her suit jacket, and hung herself from the bridge like a spider. This scared Alice so much she immediately began publishing Stein's work herself.

✧

Geography and Plays . . . Ladies Voices . . . Pink Melon Joy . . . If You Had Three Husbands . . . Advertisements . . . Scenes, Actions and Dispositions of Relations and Positions . . . A Long Gay Book . . .

✧

In the evenings Stein sat in their Paris studio beneath her portrait done by Picasso and talked to the artists, writers, and musicians who dropped by. The studio: one room in a four-room apartment on the Rue de Fleurs. Paintings on every wall, one above another, all the way to the ceiling. Stein's studio platform: a low chair, the fabric designed by Picasso, hand-stitched by Alice.

Everyone came by, especially writers. The French poet, Cocteau. The Americans—Fitzgerald, William Carlos Williams, Hemingway, Dos Passos. All wanted her acknowledgement, her blessing. She said to Hemingway: Remarks are not literature. Advised him to quit the newspaper business and get on with *The Sun Also Rises.* Later, she said he failed as a novelist because he couldn't handle time; his training in journalism had ruined him for art.

The worst thing Stein could say to you was that she wasn't interested in your work.

The worst thing Alice could do to you was not invite you back.

Everyone remembered Stein's laugh: deep, rich, a contralto's voice.

Alice never laughed; she was too busy tending guests, shopping at the market. Stein can laugh for us both, she once said in an interview: laughing is Stein's domain; silence and reverie are mine.

✧

Tender Buttons . . . Susie Asado . . . A Movie . . . .A Saint In Seven . . . Portrait of Mabel Dodge . . .

✧

Alice dusted the pictures. The Picassos, Matisses, Cezannes, Renoirs. The Grecos, Toulouse-Lautrecs, Daumiers, and a moderate-sized Gauguin.

She was small, exotically dark, wore gypsy rings and tapestry shawls. She was famous for her recipes, she had thousands of them—for eggs, for veal. Specializing in sauces made of butter, egg yolks, sugar, vermouth.

She said she had only met three real geniuses in her life: Picasso; Alfred North Whitehead; and Stein. She did not say how she knew they were geniuses.

The wives of geniuses, near-geniuses, and might-be-geniuses that I have sat with! she said.

In her kitchen the artists' wives were served their tea.

Chinese tea, lightly fragranced.

✧

Stein wrote in longhand. Alice organized and typed the

manuscripts, first on a small French portable, then on a sturdy Smith Premier. She suppressed publication of a first novel because it was about a love affair Stein had had with another woman.

After this novel, Stein kept passion strictly out of art. It does not belong there directly, she said. But it's there, oh yes, it's there, early on, and later it's there: anger, joy. She had her romantic moments. ("Lifting Belly" was a love song.) In fact, she had a "Romantic Period" during the twenties. This was after her "Spanish Period," and before the later and more accessible "Elucidation Period."

Alice's periods were of a sensual nature: her "Egyptian Head Dress Period," her "Blue Glass Bead Period," her "White Wine With Breakfast Period." And for the lonely twenty years she served as a widow after Stein's death, her "Bleak Letter Writing Period."

The summers in the south of France, the Paris studio. Stein's Model T. The trips to Spain. Years of this. Stein and Alice living on an allowance from Stein's brother Leo. Their ambulance work in France during the First World War. Their many friends amongst the GIs. Stein's few supporters; her many platforms falling into disrepair. The sale of paintings to help pay the rent, publish the books.

Occasionally Stein would succumb to the public ridicule, the constant rejection of her work. Alice would find her, mid-afternoon, collapsed on the studio couch, lying fetally, uncomfortably on her side. For a heavy woman, looking very small.

Anything you create you want to exist, she told Alice. Being in print is how my creations live. They are trying to destroy my children.

Alice told her: There's a vacant lot filled with wooden planks down on the Rue de Christine and it's a fine day for building a platform.

✧

Summer, 1926, the south of France. Stein took Alice by the hand. Led her to a meadow where they made love. All afternoon they lay on the grass, hearing nothing but the wind, the murmur of bees, the rush of low-flying birds. Alice was nervous lest they be found in so revealing a situation. But Stein was calm, smiling up at the wide blue sky, Alice's head on her lap. My wife, Stein whispered, my beautiful, beautiful wife.

That enormous presence with the dainty hands, the small neat head. Alice called her Baby.

✧

An Acquaintance With Description . . . Four Saints in Three Acts . . . Lucy Church Amiably . . . A Valentine to Sherwood Anderson . . .

✧

Each October, for forty years, they celebrated their anniversary by taking tea in Montmartre. Then a stroll through the Luxembourg Gardens.

Alice always gave Stein a gift, something she had made herself—a hat, gloves, silk-lined underwear. Or a broach. Alice was fond of amber and things caught in glass—feathers, stones, lace.

On their anniversary, Stein presented Alice with a New Work, untyped: *Wars I have Seen . . . Everybody's Autobiography . . . A Water-fall and A Piano. . . .* Written on the sly, without Alice's knowledge. The weeks leading up to the presentation filled with excitement, anticipation, joy.

Stein's pet name for Alice was Pussy.

✧

Grant or Rutherford B. Hayes . . . Page IX *. . . The Superstitions of Fred Anneday, Annday, Anday; A Novel of Real Life . . . Ida . . . Is Dead . . . The Autobiography of Alice B. Toklas . . . How Writing is Written . . . Wars I Have Seen . . .*

✧

The triumphant American tour in 1934. Stein was famous now, after publishing *The Autobiography of Alice B. Toklas* in 1932. The headlines said: GERTY GERTY STEIN IS BACK HOME HOME BACK. She'd been away for thirty years. Travelling first class with her wife, Alice, aboard the SS Champlain; they had flowers in their cabin from the Duchesse de Clermont Tonnerre, were asked to dine at the Captain's table but declined. A small child whom they met onboard is rumoured to have said that she liked the man, but why did the lady have a moustache? In New York they found themselves bombarded by reporters and cameramen. Stein loved the attention. When a reporter asked, Miss Stein, Why don't you write the way you talk?, Stein replied, Why don't you read the way I write?

For the trip Alice made Stein a leather case in which to carry her lecture notes. Also a copy of a hat that belonged to Louis XIII. There's a picture of them taken on the deck of the Champlain. Stein is wearing this hat, a somewhat unremarkable hat, close fitting with a small brim. In the picture, Alice is shown carrying both her and Stein's handbags; she has a defiant look on her face. And, yes, you can see her moustache.

✧

I Came and Here I Am . . . Answers to the Partisan Review . . . The New Hope in Our "Sad Young Men" . . . Off We All Went to See Germany . . . All About Money . . .

✧

In the mornings, if it was summer, Alice gathered strawberries for Stein's breakfast. From the market if they were in Paris, or from the garden beside their country home. (Stein never arose before noon.)

Then, together at the breakfast table: a bowl of berries, followed by eggs Benedict, fresh bread, and strong coffee. Sun through the window; rays of sunlight shining on the table, on their bent heads, like a still life. A vase of flowers, the morning papers. A breeze through the open window. And Stein and Alice talking quietly, their intimacy with words. The plans for the day. A walk, perhaps, a manuscript to type.

They spoke to each other in perfect tenses, abhorring adverbs, weaving their profound repetitions, never saying the same thing twice, a living speech.

About Stein's perfect present, her friend, Bernard Fay, had said: Her life and her work are as pleasant as a cold bath in the heat of summer.

✧

Stein said: Dead is dead. Anyone is living who has not come to be dead.

Alice said: Baby was my life.

Three

IN MEMORY OF DAVID UU

COVERS

The children do not yet know what goes on beneath the bed covers but we visit there regularly because that is where the airport is located and as you get older the flights you can take there become more and more appealing for example the Adulterous Affair Flight where finally after running through a field of gummy genitalia you land in the arms of your lover only to find that as you kiss she shrinks beneath your arms to the size of a baby doll with grotesque lips and gigantic vulva or the Rescue Flight where you are crossing a bridge to a waiting car and suddenly the bridge gives way leaving you dangling above a churning sea of red jello just barely able to hang on to a loosening board and will the helicopter arrive in time? or the flight of frustration, the Vampire With Enormous Penis Flight, where you and the vampire are caught in the same forest at daybreak but all he is interested in is finding a grave for the day and soaring through the trees with a paper bag over his head trying to dodge the flocks of crucifixes sweeping through the dawn light show or attending the Catholic Church Flight which is located in a busy gift shop crammed with ornaments collecting dust where you have a combination orgasm and religious experience while spaced every ten feet around you is a bird bath funeral pyre where priests are throwing incense on the burning bones of birds or the Naturally Occurring Surrealism Flight where you are the custodian of a prisoner of war camp for flies housed in a tiny medieval castle made of styrofoam and cardboard in which hundreds of dead or dying flies lounge in mayonaisse jars and are given room numbers room service the penthouse suite water sugar the whole works to die in imprisoned splendour and you like your work you really do

WINDOW

We moved our bed beside the window looking out across the field to the giant TV screen playing ancient love films in green and grey an old drive-in theatre and hungry for the commercials we were the hot dogs on legs being squeezed by happy ketchup and mustard bottles and the intermission sign the huge clock ticking down our time living in intermission we were and no more searching for a place to burrow into with finding our woolly nest and staying put and you naked beneath the two quilts wrapping me round and round and I in my flannelette nightgown wrapping you back with our holding on to each other before the ancient love films safe from time whirling by this splendid huddle this reprieve from what's to come

BED

Who are all these dead people at the foot of my bed? they're shoving one another three old women and a small skinny boy all trying to push one another off my bed the boy is crying shrieking why does no one come? four dead people shouldn't be here they should be on their own beds I'd get up and bite them but I haven't got the strength why won't they leave me alone? they're laughing at me crawling up the bed trying to get my purse I'm scared if I shout they'll grab me push me into the sea the sky overhead is blue I'm sitting in a deck chair beside my mother she's wearing pearls a summer's dress smile she's saying you needn't look so glum life's a song there's still time left to sing it overhead a spotlight maybe that's the sun I'm old my eyesight blurs no it's a light switching on switching off don't tell me the dead don't speak my mother's standing at the foot of my bed hold my hand she's saying the journey ahead is smooth and long there are four dead people in a row-boat bobbing in the sea hurry up jump in they're calling why does no one come? I wish the dead were people I knew instead the light keeps switching on switching off my mother's swimming towards the foot of my bed come on come on I can't swim past these pillows I'm crying I haven't got the strength my mother's in the water waving splashing the water feels so warm come on you silly girl jump in the dead are cheering wildly mouths of rust at me mouths of dust it's time it's time it's time

Green Plastic Buddha

How to keep going considering the arbitrary nature of the world. That's the problem. I look for signs. Yesterday I found a pen on Beacon Avenue outside Cornish's Book and Stationery. A white Bic taped over with Dennison Pres-A-Ply. The writing on it said, "My Science Project Sucks Shit." Surely, a message from the spheres.

I'm always bargaining with chance. It's an addiction like teenage masturbation, you're always promising yourself that this is the last time. If I empty the sink of water before the kettle boils. . . . If I make it to the stop sign before that man crosses the street. . . . Grovelling for trivial favours. I can't help fiddling with the inevitable.

That time I traded Christmas crackers with my aunt, it

was a mix-up, she sat at my place so I sat at hers. Then we opened the crackers. She got the skull-and-crossbones key chain, I got the green plastic Buddha, though both our paper hats were blue. Eight months later she died. It didn't matter that she was an old woman. What mattered was that she got the sign, not me.

Today we talked about renewing the mortgage on the house and you said it depresses you to think of a twenty-five-year amortization rate because in twenty-five years you'll be dead. You're sure of it while with each birthday I've come to place my age at exactly half of what I'll be when I die and I keep dying older and older. When I wait for our son after school I count the seconds until I see him come out of the portable. I make myself count slowly, calculating how many years I've got left. If it's a good day I make it to forty-six but most days I cheat, pretend I haven't seen him running behind a group of kids at count fifteen or twenty-three. Eternity is not something I'm after.

I use the Bic pen from Beacon Avenue to do accounting. It's not by chance that when I'm not working with words, I work with numbers. There's something solemn about movement in a closed system. Those rows and columns of quiet black numbers have a beauty all their own. I'm always surprised at which numbers dominate the day. Sometimes it's fours and sixes, sometimes it's eights, nines and twos, running like pure, emotionless currents through the page. Each story, each piece of fiction I write is an attempt to defer eternity and we all know what eternity is: it's the silence beyond time, it's that place where we have nothing to cling to.

ATTIC

The green plastic Buddha sits on my desk, scotch-taped to a rock you brought back from the beach, its gaping, idiot face still saving me from nothing.

M.A.C. FARRANT is the author of two previous fiction collections: *Sick Pigeon* (Thistledown, 1991), which was shortlisted for the Ethel Wilson Fiction Prize and the Commonwealth Writer's Prize for First Book; and *Raw Material* (Arsenal Pulp Press, 1993), shortlisted for the VanCity Women's Book Prize. She lives in Sidney, B.C.